ERLE STANLEY GARDNER

- Cited by the *Guinness Book of World Records* as the #1 bestselling writer of all time!

- Author of more than 150 clever, authentic, and sophisticated mystery novels!

- Creator of the amazing Perry Mason, the savvy Della Street, and dynamite detective Paul Drake!

- **THE ONLY AUTHOR WHO OUTSELLS AGATHA CHRISTIE, HAROLD ROBBINS, BARBARA CARTLAND, AND LOUIS L'AMOUR *COMBINED!***

Why?

Because he writes the best, most fascinating whodunits of all!

You'll want to read every one of them,
from
BALLANTINE BOOKS

D1449712

Also by Erle Stanley Gardner
Published by Ballantine Books:

The Case of the
Lucky Loser

Erle Stanley Gardner

BALLANTINE BOOKS · NEW YORK

An abridged version of this book has appeared serially in *The Saturday Evening Post*.

ISBN 0-345-36497-X

This edition published by arrangement with William Morrow and Company, Inc.

Manufactured in the United States of America

First Ballantine Books Edition: February 1990

Foreword

Nearly a year ago my good friend John Ben Shepperd, the Attorney General of the State of Texas, told me, "The next big development in law enforcement must come from the people rather than from the police."

General Shepperd wasn't content with merely predicting such a development. He discussed it with several influential businessmen in Texas, and soon these businessmen began to take action.

J. Marion West of Houston, Texas, affectionately known as "Silver Dollar" West, is an attorney at law, a cattleman, an oil operator, and is widely respected for his knowledge of police science. He spends a large portion of his time assisting local police officers in the Houston area.

I have for some years been associated with Park Street, who is a member of "The Court of Last Resort," a San Antonio attorney with driving energy, and a boundless enthusiasm for his work. Park Street has as his lifetime ambition a desire to improve the administration of justice.

Jackson B. Love, of Llano, Texas, is an ex-Texas Ranger who has had considerable experience as a peace officer. He owns and operates a large ranch, has exceptionally sound business judgment, is quite an historian, and collects books dealing with the frontier period of the West.

W. R. (Billy Bob) Crim, of Kilgore, Texas, a man with extensive oil interests in Kilgore, Longview and Dallas, is vitally interested in state police work and is an authority on weapons.

Frederick O. Detweiler, president of Chance Vought Aircraft, Incorporated, Dallas, Texas, is representative of the modern executive, with broad interests, a razor-keen mind and a background of knowledge ranging from economics to public relations. He is one of the prominent businessmen of Texas and is known and loved all over the state for his intense interest in better law enforcement.

Dr. Merton M. Minter is a prominent physician of San Antonio, a man loved and respected by those who know him. Recently he began to take an active interest in law enforcement. A member of the Board of Regents of the University of Texas, he is particularly interested in the educational aspects of crime prevention and law enforcement.

These people got together with Attorney General John Ben Shepperd and decided to organize the Texas Law Enforcement Foundation, of which my good friend Park Street is Chairman and J. Marion (Jim) West is Vice-chairman.

When Texas does anything, it does it in a big way, and this Law Enforcement Foundation is no exception.

Col. Homer Garrison, Jr., Director of the Texas Department of Public Safety, and as such, head of the famed Texas Rangers, a man who is acclaimed everywhere as one of the outstanding figures in the field of executive law enforcement, is Chairman of the Advisory Council of the Foundation.

I consider myself greatly honored in that I have been appointed a special adviser of this Foundation.

The Texas Law Enforcement Foundation isn't a "Crime Commission." Its primary purpose is to acquaint citizens everywhere with their civic responsibilities in the field of law enforcement. The Foundation wants the average citizen to have a better understanding of the causes of crime, of how crime can be prevented, of the responsibilities of the police officer, the latent dangers of juvenile delinquency, the purpose and problems of penology, and the responsibilities of the organized bar and of lawyers generally.

If the average citizen can't learn more about the problems with which the various law enforcement agencies have to contend, the citizen can't play his part in the job of curtailing crime.

As of this writing, organized crime is making an alarming bid for power. Juvenile delinquency is but little understood and is on the increase.

On many fronts we are trying to combat atomic age crime methods with horse-and-buggy thinking.

Efficient law enforcement can't function in a civic vacuum. The police force depends on the training, integrity and loyalty of its members for efficiency, and on public understanding and cooperation for its very life.

It is well known that if the average community had half as much loyalty to its police as the police have to the community we would have far less crime.

Because I consider the work of this law enforcement foundation so important, I have departed from my usual custom of dedicating books to outstanding figures in the field of legal medicine, and I dedicate this book to those citizens of Texas who, at great personal and financial sacrifice, have been responsible for bringing into existence a new concept of law enforcement.

—Erle Stanley Gardner

Since this Foreword was written in 1956, J. Marion West has died. His contributions are greatly missed. John Ben Shepperd is no longer Attorney General of the State of Texas but remains actively interested in the program.

Temecula, 1958

CAST OF CHARACTERS

Chapter 1

Della Street, Perry Mason's confidential secretary, picked up the telephone and said, "Hello."

The well-modulated youthful voice of a woman asked, "How much does Mr. Mason charge for a day in court?"

Della Street's voice reflected cautious appraisal of the situation. "That would depend very much on the type of case, what he was supposed to do and—"

"He won't be supposed to do anything except listen."

"You mean you wouldn't want him to take part in the trial?"

"No. Just listen to what goes on in the courtroom and draw conclusions."

"Who is this talking, please?"

"Would you like the name that will appear on your books?"

"Certainly."

"Cash."

"What?"

"Cash."

"I think you'd better talk to Mr. Mason," Della Street said. "I'll try to arrange an appointment."

"There isn't time for that. The case in which I am interested starts at ten o'clock this morning."

"Just a moment, please. Hold the wire," Della Street said.

She entered Mason's private office.

Perry Mason looked up from the mail he was reading.

Della Street said, "Chief, you'll have to handle this personally. A youthful-sounding woman wants to retain you to

1

sit in court today just to listen to a case. She's on the phone now.''

''What's her name?''

''She says it's Cash.''

Mason grinned, picked up his telephone. Della Street got on the other line, put through the connection.

''Yes?'' Mason said crisply. ''This is Perry Mason.''

The woman's voice was silky. ''There's a criminal case on trial in Department Twenty-three of the Superior Court entitled People versus Balfour. I would like to know how much it's going to cost me to have you attend court during the day, listen to the proceedings, and then give me your conclusions.''

''And your name?'' Mason asked.

''As I told your secretary, the name is Cash—just the way the entry will appear on your books.''

Mason looked at his watch. ''It is now nine twenty-five. I have two appointments this morning and one this afternoon. I would have to cancel those appointments, and I would only do that to handle a matter of the greatest importance.''

''This *is* a matter of the greatest importance.''

''My charges would be predicated upon that fact, upon the necessity of breaking three appointments and—''

''Just what would your charges be?'' she asked.

''Five hundred dollars,'' Mason snapped.

The voice suddenly lost its silky assurance. ''Oh! . . . I . . . I'm sorry. I had no idea. . . . We'll just have to forget it, I guess. I'm sorry.''

Mason, moved by the consternation in the young woman's voice, said, ''More than you expected?''

''Y . . . y . . . yes.''

''How much more?''

''I . . . I . . . I work on a salary and . . . well, I—''

''You see,'' Mason explained, ''I have to pay salaries, taxes, office rental, and I have a law library to keep up. And a day of my time— What sort of work do *you* do?''

''I'm a secretary.''

"And you want me just to listen to this case?"

"I did . . . I guess I . . . I mean, my ideas were all out of line."

"What had you expected to pay?"

"I had hoped you'd say a hundred dollars. I could have gone for a hundred and fifty . . . Well, I'm sorry."

"Why did you want me to listen? Are you interested in the case?"

"Not directly, no."

"Do you have a car?"

"No."

"Any money in the bank?"

"Yes."

"How much?"

"A little over six hundred."

"All right," Mason said. "You've aroused my curiosity. If you'll pay me a hundred dollars I'll go up and listen."

"Oh, Mr. Mason! . . . Oh . . . thanks! I'll send a messenger right up. You see, you mustn't ever know who I am. . . . I can't explain. The money will be delivered at once."

"Exactly what is it you want me to do?" Mason asked.

"Please don't let *anyone* know that you have been retained in this case. I would prefer that you go as a spectator and that you do not sit in the bar reserved for attorneys."

"Suppose I can't find a seat?" Mason asked.

"I've thought of that," she said. "When you enter the courtroom, pause to look around. A woman will be seated in the left-hand aisle seat, fourth row back. She is a red-haired woman about . . . well, she's in her forties. Next to her will be a younger woman with dark chestnut hair, and next to her will be a seat on which will be piled a couple of coats. The younger woman will pick up the coats and you may occupy that seat. Let's hope you aren't recognized. Please *don't* carry a brief case."

There was a very decisive click at the other end of the line.

Mason turned to Della Street.

"When that messenger comes in with the hundred dollars, Della, be sure that he takes a receipt, and tell him to deliver that receipt to the person who gave him the money. I'm on my way to court."

Chapter 2

Perry Mason reached the courtroom of Department Twenty-three just as Judge Mervin Spencer Cadwell was entering from his chambers.

The bailiff pounded his gavel. "Everybody rise," he shouted.

Mason took advantage of the momentary confusion to slip down the center aisle to the fourth row of seats.

The bailiff called court to order. Judge Cadwell seated himself. The bailiff banged the gavel. The spectators dropped back to their seats, and Mason unostentatiously stepped across in front of the two women.

The younger woman deftly picked up two coats which were on the adjoining seat. Mason sat down, glancing surreptitiously at the women as he did so.

The women were both looking straight ahead, apparently paying not the slightest attention to him.

Judge Cadwell said, "People of the State of California versus Theodore Balfour. Is it stipulated by counsel that the jurors are all present and the defendant is in court?"

"So stipulated, Your Honor."

"Proceed."

"I believe the witness George Dempster was on the stand," the prosecutor said.

"That's right," Judge Cadwell said. "Mr. Dempster, will you please return to the stand."

George Dempster, a big-boned, slow-moving man in his thirties, took the witness stand.

"Now, you testified yesterday that you found certain pieces of glass near the body on the highway?" the prosecutor asked.

"That is right, yes, sir."

"And did you have occasion to examine the headlights on the automobile which you located in the Balfour garage?"

"I did, yes, sir."

"What was the condition of those headlights?"

"The right headlight was broken."

"When did you make your examination?"

"About seven-fifteen on the morning of the twentieth."

"Did you ask permission from anyone to make this examination?"

"No, sir, not to examine the car itself."

"Why not?"

"Well, we wanted to check before we committed ourselves."

"So what did you do?"

"We went out to the Balfour residence. There was a four-car garage in back. There was no sign of life in the house, but someone was moving around in an apartment over the garage. As we drove in, this person looked out of the window and then came down the stairs. He identified himself as a servant who had one of the apartments over the garage. I told him that we were officers and we wanted to look around in the garage, that we were looking for some evidence of a crime. I asked him if he had any objection. He said certainly not, so we opened the garage door and went in."

"Now, directing your attention to a certain automobile bearing license number GMB 665, I will ask you if you found anything unusual about that car?"

"Yes, sir, I did."

"What did you find?"

"I found a broken right front headlight, a very slight dent on the right side of the front of the car, and I found a few spatters of blood on the bumper."

"What did you do next?"

"I told the servant we would have to impound the car and that we wanted to question the person who'd been driving it. I asked him who owned it, and he said Mr. Guthrie Balfour owned it, but that his nephew, Ted Balfour, had been driving—"

"Move to strike," the defense attorney snapped. "Hearsay, incompetent, irrelevant, immaterial. They can't prove who drove the car by hearsay."

"Motion granted," Judge Cadwell said. "The prosecution knows it can't use evidence of that sort."

"I'm sorry, Your Honor," the prosecutor said. "I was about to stipulate that part of the answer could go out. We had not intended to prove who was driving in this way. The witness should understand that.

"Now just tell the Court and the jury what you did after that, Mr. Dempster."

"We got young Mr. Balfour up out of bed."

"Now, when you refer to young Mr. Balfour, you are referring to the defendant in this case?"

"That's right. Yes, sir."

"Did you have a conversation with him?"

"Yes, sir."

"At what time?"

"Well, by the time we had this conversation it was right around eight o'clock."

"You got him up out of bed?"

"Somebody awakened him, he put on a bathrobe and came out. We told him who we were and what we wanted, and he said he wouldn't talk with us until he was dressed and had had his coffee."

"What did you do?"

"Well, we tried to get something out of him. We tried to be nice about it. We didn't want to throw our weight around, but he kept saying he wouldn't talk until he'd had his coffee."

"Where did this conversation take place?"

"At the Guthrie Balfour residence."

"And who was present at that conversation?"

"Another police officer who had gone out with me, a Mr. Dawson."

"He is here in court?"

"Yes, sir."

"Who else was present?"

"The defendant."

"Anyone else?"

"No, sir."

"Where did that conversation take place?"

"In the house."

"I mean specifically where in the house?"

"In a small office, sort of a study that opened off from the defendant's bedroom. The butler or somebody had brought up some coffee, cream and sugar and the morning paper, and we drank coffee—"

"You say '*we* drank coffee'?"

"That's right. The butler brought in three cups and saucers, cream, sugar, and a big electric percolator. We all three had coffee."

"Now, just what did you say to the defendant and what did he say to you?"

Mortimer Dean Howland, the attorney representing Balfour, was on his feet. "I object, Your Honor. No proper foundation has been laid."

Judge Cadwell pursed his lips, looked down at the witness, then at the prosecutor.

"And," Howland went on, "I feel that I should be entitled to cross-examine this witness before any admission, confession, or declaration by the defendant is received in evidence."

"We're not laying the foundation for a confession, Your Honor," the prosecutor said.

"That's precisely my objection," the defense attorney remarked.

Judge Cadwell gave the matter careful consideration.

Mason took advantage of the opportunity to study the young woman on his right. Having saved a seat for him, she must have known he was to be there. Having known that, the chances were she was the woman who had sent him the retainer.

"What's the case?" Mason asked her in a whisper.

She looked at him coldly, elevated her chin and turned away.

It was the man on Mason's left who tersely said, "Hit and run, manslaughter."

Judge Cadwell said, "I will accept the prosecutor's assurance that no confession is called for by this question and overrule the objection. The witness will answer the question."

The witness said, "He said he'd been seeing his uncle and his uncle's wife off on a train, that he'd then gone to a party, where he'd had a few drinks and—"

"Just a moment, Your Honor, just a moment," the defense attorney interrupted. "It now appears that the statement by the prosecutor was incorrect, that they *are* attempting to establish a confession or an admission and—"

"I'm going to ask the prosecutor about this," Judge Cadwell interrupted sternly.

The prosecutor was on his feet. "Please, Your Honor. If you will listen to the answer, you will understand my position."

"There is an admission?" Judge Cadwell asked.

"Certainly, Your Honor, but an admission does not rank in the same category with a confession."

"They are attempting to show that he confessed to being drunk," the defense attorney said.

"I'll let the witness finish his answer," Judge Cadwell said. "Go on."

"The defendant said that he'd had a few drinks at this party and had become ill. He thought at least one of the drinks had been loaded. He said he passed out and remembered nothing until he came to in his automobile, that—"

"Your Honor, Your Honor!" the defense attorney protested. "This now has the very definite earmarks of—"

"Sit down," Judge Cadwell said. "Let the witness finish his answer. If the answer is as I think it's going to be, I am then going to call on the prosecutor for an explanation. The

9

Court doesn't like this. The Court feels that an attempt has been made to impose on the Court."

"If you will only hear the answer out," the prosecutor pleaded.

"That's exactly what I'm going to do."

"Go ahead," the prosecutor said to the witness.

The witness continued, "He said that for a brief instant he came to his senses in his car, that some woman was driving."

"Some *woman*?" Judge Cadwell exclaimed.

"Yes, Your Honor."

"Then *he* wasn't driving?"

"That's right, Your Honor," the prosecutor said. "I trust the Court will now see the reason for my statement."

"Very well," Judge Cadwell said. He turned to the witness. "Go on. What else did the defendant say?"

"He said that he partially revived for a moment, that he remembered being very sick, that the next thing he remembered he was home and in bed, that he had a terrific thirst, that the hour was four thirty-five in the morning, that he was conscious but very thick-headed."

"Did you ask him who the woman was who was driving the car?" the prosecutor asked the witness.

"I did."

"What did he say?"

"He said he couldn't remember, that he couldn't be certain."

"Which did he say—that he couldn't remember or he couldn't be certain?"

"He said both."

"What did you ask him?"

"I asked him several questions after that, but I had no more answers. He wanted to know what had happened. I told him that we were investigating a death, a hit-and-run case, and that there was some evidence his car had been involved. So then he said if that was the case he would say nothing more until he had consulted with his attorney."

"You may cross-examine," the prosecutor said.

Mortimer Dean Howland, attorney for Balfour, was known for his hammer-and-tongs, browbeating cross-examination.

He lowered his bushy eyebrows, thrust out his jaw, glared for a moment at the witness, said, "You went out to that house to get a confession from the defendant, didn't you?"

"I did nothing of the sort."

"You *did* go out to the house?"

"Certainly."

"And you *did* try to get a confession from the defendant?"

"Yes, in a way."

"So then you did go out to that house to try and get a confession from the defendant—either by one way or another!"

"I went out to look at the defendant's automobile."

"*Why* did you decide to go out to look at the defendant's automobile?"

"Because of something I had been told."

The lawyer hesitated, then, fearing to open that legal door, abruptly changed his tactics. "When you *first* saw the defendant, you wakened him from a sound sleep, didn't you?"

"*I* didn't. The servant did."

"You knew that he had been ill?"

"He looked as though he'd had a hard night. That was all I knew until he told me he'd been sick. I thought that he—"

"Never mind what you thought!" Howland shouted.

"I thought that's what you asked for," the witness said calmly.

There was a ripple of merriment throughout the courtroom.

"Just concentrate on my questions!" Howland shouted. "You could tell that the defendant was not in good health?"

"I could tell that he wasn't fresh as a daisy. He looked like a man with a terrific hangover."

"I didn't ask you that. I asked you if you couldn't tell that he wasn't in good health."

"He wasn't in good spirits, but he sure looked as though he *had* been in spirits."

"That will do," Howland said. "Don't try to be facetious. A man's liberty is at stake here. Simply answer the questions. You knew that he wasn't his normal self?"

"I don't know what he's like when he's normal."

"You knew that he had been aroused from sleep?"

"I assumed that he had."

"You knew that he didn't look well?"

"That's right."

"How did he look?"

"He looked terrible. He looked like a man with a hangover."

"You've seen men with hangovers?"

"Lots of them."

"Have *you* ever had a hangover?"

"Your Honor, I object to that," the prosecutor said.

Howland said, "Then I move to strike out the answer of the witness that the defendant had a hangover on the ground that it is a conclusion of the witness, that the answer is merely an opinion, and that the witness is not properly qualified to give that opinion."

"I'll withdraw the objection," the prosecutor said.

"Have *you* ever had a hangover?"

"No."

"You have *never* had a hangover?"

"No."

"You're not a drinking man?"

"I'm not a teetotaler. I take a drink once in a while. I can't ever remember being intoxicated. I can't ever remember having had a hangover."

"Then how do you know what a man with a hangover looks like?"

"I have seen men with hangovers."

"What is a hangover?"

"The aftermath of an intoxicated condition. I may say it's

the immediate aftermath of an intoxicated condition when the alcohol has not entirely left the system."

"You're now talking like a doctor."

"You asked me for my definition of a hangover."

"Oh, that's all," Howland said, making a gesture of throwing up his hands as though tired of arguing, and turned his back on the witness.

The witness started to leave the stand.

"Just a moment," Howland said suddenly, whirling and leveling an extended forefinger. "One more question. Did the defendant tell you what time it was that he passed out?"

"He *said* about ten o'clock."

"Oh, he said about ten o'clock, did he?"

"Yes, sir."

"You didn't tell us that before."

"I wasn't asked."

"You were asked to tell what the defendant told you, weren't you?"

"Yes."

"Then why did you try to conceal this statement about its being near ten o'clock?"

"I . . . well, I didn't pay much attention to that."

"Why not?"

"Frankly, I didn't believe it."

"Did you believe his story about some woman driving his car?"

"No."

"Yet you paid attention to that part of his statement?"

"Well, yes. That was different."

"In what way?"

"Well, that was an admission."

"You mean an admission adverse to the interests of the defendant?"

"Certainly."

"Oh! So you went there prepared to remember any admissions the defendant might make and to forget anything he might say that was in his favor, is that it?"

"I didn't forget this. I simply didn't mention it because I wasn't asked the specific question which would call for it."

"What time were you called to investigate the hit-and-run accident?"

"About two o'clock in the morning."

"The body was lying on the highway?"

"Yes, sir."

"How long had it been there?"

"I don't know of my own knowledge."

"Do you know when it was reported to the police?"

"Yes."

"When?"

"About fifteen minutes before we got there."

"That was a well-traveled highway?"

"It was a surfaced road. There was some traffic over it."

"The body couldn't have been there on such a well-traveled road more than ten or fifteen minutes without someone having reported it?"

"I don't know."

"It's a well-traveled road?"

"Yes."

"And the defendant was driven home at about ten o'clock?"

"That's what he said."

"And he was ill?"

"That's what he said."

"And went to bed?"

"That's what he said."

The lawyer hesitated. "And went to sleep?"

"He didn't say that. He said his mind was a blank until he came to around four-thirty in the morning."

"He didn't say his mind was a blank, did he?"

"He said he couldn't remember."

"Didn't he say that the next thing he knew he came to in bed?"

"He said the next thing he *remembered* he was in bed, and it was then four thirty-five in the morning."

14

"But some of what the defendant told you you didn't remember—everything he said that was in his favor."

"I told you I did remember it."

"And neglected to tell us."

"All right. Have it that way if you want it that way."

"Oh, that's all," Howland said. "In view of your very apparent bias, I don't care to ask you any more questions."

The witness glared angrily and left the stand.

The prosecutor said, "No redirect examination. Call Myrtle Anne Haley."

The redheaded woman who was seated on the aisle two seats over from Perry Mason got up, walked to the witness stand, held up her right hand, and was sworn.

Mason stole a surreptitious glance at the young woman sitting next to him.

She held her chin in the air, giving him only her profile to look at. Her expression held the icy disdain that a young woman reserves for someone who is trying to pick her up and is being offensive about it.

Chapter 3

Myrtle Anne Haley took the oath, gave her name and address to the court reporter, and settled herself in the witness chair with the manner of one who knows her testimony is going to be decisive.

The prosecutor said, "I call your attention to the road map which has been previously identified and introduced in evidence as People's Exhibit A, Mrs. Haley."

"Yes, sir."

"Do you understand that map? That is, are you familiar with the territory which it portrays?"

"Yes, sir."

"I call your attention to a section of Sycamore Road as shown on that map and which lies between Chestnut Street and State Highway. Do you understand that that map delineates such a section of road?"

"Yes, sir."

"Have you ever driven over that road?"

"Many times."

"Where do you live?"

"On the other side of State Highway on Sycamore Road."

"Can you show us on this map? Just make a cross on the map and circle the cross."

The witness made a cross on the map and enclosed it in a circle.

The prosecutor said, "I will call your attention to the night of the nineteenth and the morning of the twentieth of September of this year. Did you have occasion to use the highway at that time?"

16

"On the morning of the twentieth—early in the morning—yes, sir."

"At what time?"

"Between twelve-thirty and one-thirty."

"In the morning?"

"Yes, sir."

"In which direction were you driving?"

"Going west on Sycamore Road. I was approaching Chestnut Street from the east."

"And did you notice anything unusual at that time?"

"Yes, sir. A car ahead of me which was being driven in a very erratic manner."

"Can you tell me more about the erratic manner in which the car was being driven?"

"Well, it was weaving about the road, crossing the center line and going clear over to the left. Then it would go back to the right and at times would run clear off the highway on the right side."

"Could you identify that car?"

"Yes. I wrote down the license number."

"Then what?"

"Then I followed along behind; then at this wide place in the road about four-fifths of the way to State Highway I shot on by."

"You say you *shot* on by?"

"Well, I went by fast when I had a chance. I didn't want the driver to swerve into me."

"I move to strike everything about why she passed the car," Howland said.

"That will go out," Judge Cadwell said.

"After you got by the car what did you do?"

"I went home and went to bed."

"I mean immediately after you got by the car. Did you do anything?"

"I looked in the rearview mirror."

"And what did you see, if anything?"

"I saw the car swerve over to the left, then back to the

right, and all of a sudden I saw something black cross in front of the headlights, and then for a moment the right headlight seemed to go out.''

''You say it *seemed* to go out?''

''After that it came on again.''

''And that was on Sycamore Road at a point between Chestnut Street and State Highway?''

''Yes, sir.''

''That is the point at which you saw the light blink off and then on?''

''Yes, sir.''

''At a time when you were looking in your rearview mirror?''

''Yes, sir.''

''And did you know what caused that headlight to seem to go out?''

''I didn't at the time, but I do now.''

''What was it?''

''Objected to as calling for a conclusion of the witness,'' Howland said. ''The question is argumentative.''

''The objection is sustained,'' Judge Cadwell said. ''The witness can testify to what she saw.''

''But, Your Honor,'' the prosecutor said, ''the witness certainly has the right to interpret what she sees.''

Judge Cadwell shook his head. ''The witness will testify to what she saw. The jury will make the interpretation.''

The prosecutor paused for a minute, then said, ''Very well. Cross-examine.''

''You took down the license number of this automobile?'' Howland asked.

''That's right.''

''In a notebook?''

''Yes.''

''Where did you get that notebook?''

''From my purse.''

''You were driving the car?''

''Yes.''

18

"Was anyone with you?"

"No."

"You took the notebook from your purse?"

"Yes."

"And a pencil?"

"Not a pencil. A fountain pen."

"And marked down the license number of the automobile?"

"Yes."

"What was that license number?"

"GMB 665."

"You have that notebook with you?"

"Yes, sir."

"I would like to see it, please."

The prosecutor smiled at the jury. "Not the slightest objection," he said. "We're very glad to let you inspect it."

Howland walked up to the witness stand, took the notebook the witness gave him, thumbed through the pages, said, "This seems to be a notebook in which you kept a lot of data, various and sundry entries."

"I don't carry anything in memory which I can trust to paper."

"Now then," Howland said, "this number, GMB 665, is the last entry in the book."

"That's right."

"That entry was made on September twentieth?"

"About twelve-thirty to one-thirty on the morning of September twentieth," the witness stated positively.

"Why haven't you made any entries after that?"

"Because, after I read about the accident, I reported to the police, the police took the book, and it was then given back to me with the statement that I should take good care of it because it would be evidence."

"I see," Howland said with elaborate politeness. "And how long did the police have the book?"

"They had the book for . . . I don't know . . . quite a while."

"And when was it given back to you?"

"Well, after the police had it, the district attorney had it."

"Oh, the police gave it to the district attorney, did they?"

"I don't know. I know the prosecutor was the one who gave it to me."

"When?"

"This morning."

"This *morning*?" Howland said, his voice showing a combination of incredulity and skeptical sarcasm. "And *why* did the prosecutor give it back to you this morning?"

"So I could have it on the witness stand."

"Oh, so you would be able to say that you had the notebook with you?"

"I don't know. I suppose that was it."

"Now then, did you remember the license number?"

"Certainly I did. Just as I told you. It's GMB 665."

"When did you last see that license number?"

"When I handed you the book just a moment ago."

"And when before that?"

"This morning."

"At what time this morning?"

"About nine o'clock this morning."

"And how long did you spend looking at that number at about nine o'clock this morning?"

"I . . . I don't know. I don't know as it makes any difference."

"Were you looking at it for half an hour?"

"Certainly not."

"For fifteen minutes?"

"No."

"For ten minutes?"

"I may have been."

"In other words, you were memorizing that number this morning, weren't you?"

"Well, what's wrong with that?"

"How do you know that's the same number?"

20

"Because that's my handwriting, that's the number just as I wrote it down."

"Could you see the license number of the car ahead while you were writing this?"

"Certainly."

"All the time you were writing?"

"Yes."

"Isn't it a fact that you looked at the license number, then stopped your car, got out your notebook, and—"

"Certainly not! It's just as I told you. I took out my notebook while I was driving and wrote down the number."

"You are right-handed?"

"Yes."

"You had one hand on the wheel?"

"My left hand."

"And were writing with your right hand?"

"Yes."

"Do you have a fountain pen or a ball-point pen?"

"It's a plain fountain pen."

"The top screws off?"

"Yes."

"And you unscrewed that with one hand?"

"Certainly."

"You can do that with one hand?"

"Of course. You hold the pen . . . that is, the barrel of the pen with the last two fingers, then use the thumb and forefinger to unscrew the cap."

"Then what did you do?"

"I put the notebook down on my lap, wrote the number, then put the cap back on the pen and put the notebook and fountain pen back in my purse."

"How far were you from the automobile when you were writing down this number?"

"Not very far."

"Did you see the number all the time?"

"Yes."

"Plainly?"

"Yes."

"Did you write this number in the dark?"

"No."

"No, apparently not. The number is neatly written. You must have had some light when you wrote it."

"I did. I switched on the dome light so I could see what I was writing."

"Now then," Howland said, "if you had to memorize that number this morning *after* the prosecutor had given you your notebook, you didn't know what that number was *before* he gave you the notebook, did you?"

"Well . . . you can't expect a person to remember a number all that time."

"So you didn't know what it was this morning?"

"After I'd seen the book."

"But not before that?"

"Well . . . no."

Howland hesitated for a moment. "After you had written down this number you drove on home?"

"Yes."

"Did you call the police?"

"Certainly. I told you I did."

"When?"

"Later."

"After you had read in the newspaper about this accident?"

"Yes."

"That is, about the body having been found on this road?"

"Yes."

"You didn't call the police before that?"

"No."

"Why did you write down this license number?"

Her eyes glittered with triumph. "Because I knew that the person who was driving the automobile was too drunk to have any business being behind the wheel of a car."

"You knew that when you wrote down the license number?"

"Yes."

"Then why did you write it down?"

"So I'd know what it was."

"So you could testify against the driver?"

"So I could do my duty as a citizen."

"You mean call the police?"

"Well, I thought it was my duty to make a note of the license number in case the driver got in any trouble."

"Oh, so you could testify?"

"So I could tell the police about it, yes."

"But you *didn't* tell the police until after you'd read in the paper about a body having been found?"

"That's right."

"Even after you saw this mysterious blackout of the right headlight you didn't call the police?"

"No."

"You didn't think there was any reason to call the police?"

"Not until after I'd read in the paper about the body."

"Then you *didn't* think there had been an accident when you got home, did you?"

"Well, I knew something had happened. I kept wondering what could have caused that blackout of that headlight."

"You didn't think there had been an accident?"

"I knew something had happened."

"Did you or did you not think there had been an accident?"

"Yes, I realized there must have been an accident."

"When did you realize this?"

"Right after I got home."

"And you had taken this number so you could call the police in the event of an accident?"

"I took the number because I thought it was my duty to take it . . . yes."

"Then why didn't you call the police?"

"I think this has been asked and answered several times,

Your Honor," the prosecutor said. "I dislike to curtail counsel in his cross-examination, but this certainly has been gone over repeatedly in the same way and in the same manner."

"I think so," Judge Cadwell said.

"I submit, Your Honor, that her actions contradict her words, that her reasons contradict her actions."

"You may have ample opportunity to argue the case to the jury. I believe the fact which you wished to establish by this cross-examination has been established," Judge Cadwell said.

"That's all," Howland said, shrugging his shoulders and waving his hand as though brushing the testimony to one side.

"That's all, Mrs. Haley," the prosecutor said.

Mrs. Haley swept from the witness stand, marched down the aisle, seated herself on the aisle seat.

She turned to the young woman seated beside Perry Mason. "Was I all right?" Mrs. Haley asked in a whisper.

The young woman nodded.

Judge Cadwell looked at the clock, and adjourned court until two o'clock that afternoon.

Chapter 4

During the afternoon session the prosecution tied up a few loose ends and put on a series of technical witnesses. By three-thirty the case was ready for argument.

The prosecutor made a brief, concise argument, asked for a conviction, and sat down.

Mortimer Dean Howland, a criminal attorney of the old school, indulged in a barrage of sarcasm directed at the testimony of Myrtle Anne Haley, whom he characterized as "the psychic driver," a "woman who could drive without even looking at the road."

"Notice the driving activities of this woman," Howland said. "When she first comes to our notice she is driving without looking at the road because she is getting her fountain pen and her notebook out of her purse. Then she is opening the notebook and making a note of the license number.

"Look at where she made this notation, ladies and gentlemen of the jury. She didn't open the notebook at random and scribble the license number on *any* page she happened to come to. She carefully turned to the page which contained the last notebook entry; then she neatly wrote the license number of the automobile.

"Look at this exhibit," Howland said, going over and picking up the notebook. "Look at the manner in which this number is written. Could you have written a license number so neatly if your eyes had been on the road while you were driving a car? Certainly not! Neither could this paragon of blind driving, this Myrtle Anne Haley. She was writing down

25

this number with her eyes on the page of the notebook, not on the road.

"You'll remember that I asked her on cross-examination if she had sufficient light to write by, and do you remember what she said? She said she turned on the dome light of the automobile, so that she would have plenty of light.

"*Why* did she need plenty of light? Because she was watching what she was writing, not where her car was going.

"If her eyes had been on the road, she wouldn't have needed any light in the interior of the automobile. In fact, that light would have detracted from her ability to look ahead down the road. The reason she needed light, ladies and gentlemen, was because she was driving along, looking down at the page of the notebook as she wrote.

"She was driving at an even faster rate of speed than the car ahead because she admits she *shot* past that car. *But*, ladies and gentlemen, she didn't have her eyes on the road.

"I'm willing to admit that some unfortunate person was struck by an automobile on that stretch of road. Who was more likely to have struck that person? The driver of the car ahead, or some woman who admits to you under oath that she was speeding along that road not looking where she went, with her eyes on the page of a notebook?

"And who was driving this automobile, the license number of which Myrtle Anne Haley was so careful to write down? The prosecution asked her all about the license number, but *it never asked her who was driving the car*! It never asked her even if a *man* was driving the car. For all we know, if she had been asked she may have said that a woman was driving the car."

"Your Honor," the prosecutor said, "I dislike to interrupt, but if the prosecution failed to cover that point, we ask to reopen the case at this time and ask additional questions of the witness, Myrtle Anne Haley."

"Is there any objection?" Judge Cadwell asked.

"Certainly there's an objection, Your Honor. That's an old trick, an attempt to interrupt the argument of counsel for the defense and put on more testimony. It is an attempt to distract the attention of the jury and disrupt the orderly course of trial."

"The motion is denied," Judge Cadwell said.

Howland turned to the jury, spread his hands apart and smiled. "You see, ladies and gentlemen, the sort of thing we have been up against in this case. I don't think I need to argue any more. I feel I can safely leave the matter to your discretion. I know that you will return the only fair verdict, the only just verdict, the only verdict that will enable you to feel that you have conscientiously discharged your sworn duty—a verdict of NOT GUILTY!"

Howland returned to his chair.

The prosecutor made a closing argument, the judge read instructions to the jury, and the jury retired.

Mason arose with the other spectators as court was adjourned, but Mortimer Dean Howland pushed his way to Mason's side. "Well, well, well, Counselor. What brings *you* here?"

"Picking up some pointers on how to try a case."

Howland smiled, but his eyes, gimleted in hard appraisal, burned under bushy eyebrows as they searched Mason's face.

"*You* don't need any pointers, Counselor. I thought I had glimpsed you in the crowd this morning, and then I was quite certain that you sat through the entire afternoon session. Are you interested in the case?"

"It's an interesting case."

"I mean are you interested professionally?"

"Oh, of course professionally," Mason said with expansive indefiniteness. "I don't know any of the parties. By the way, who was the person who was killed?"

"The body has never been identified," Howland said. "Fingerprints were sent to the FBI, but there was no file. The person was evidently a drifter of some sort. The head had been thrown to the highway with a terrific impact. The skull was smashed like an eggshell. Then both wheels had

27

gone completely over the head. The features were unrecognizable."

"What about the clothing?"

"Good clothing, but the labels had been carefully removed. We thought, of course, that meant the decedent might have had a criminal record. But, as I say, there were no fingerprints on file."

"Was this license number written in the notebook *immediately* under the other entries on the last page?" Mason asked.

"Come take a look," Howland invited, placing a fraternal hand on Mason's shoulder. "I'd like to have you take a look at that and tell me what *you* think."

Howland led the way to the clerk's desk. "Let's look at that exhibit," he said, ". . . the notebook."

The clerk handed him the notebook.

Mason studied the small, neat figures near the bottom of the page.

"You couldn't do that without a light to save your life," Howland said. "That woman wasn't watching the road while she was writing down the figures."

"I take it that you know the right headlight on *her* car wasn't smashed," Mason said.

"We know lots of things," Howland observed, winking. "We also know that it's an easy matter to get a headlight repaired. What's your opinion of the case, Mason? What do you think the jurors will do?"

"They may not do anything."

Howland's voice was cautious. "You think it will be a hung jury?"

"It could be."

Howland lowered his voice to a whisper. "Confidentially," he said, "that's what I was trying for. It's the best I can hope to expect."

Chapter 5

Mason sat at his desk, thoughtfully smoking. Della Street had cleaned up her secretarial desk, started for the door, returned for something which she had apparently forgotten, then she opened the drawers in her desk one after another, taking out papers, rearranging them.

Mason grinned. "Why don't you just break down and wait, Della?"

"Heavens! Was I that obvious?"

Mason nodded.

She laughed nervously. "Well, I *will* wait for a few minutes."

"The phone's plugged in through the switchboard?"

"Yes. Gertie's gone home. She left the main trunk line plugged through to your phone. In case this woman—"

Della Street broke off as the telephone rang.

Mason nodded to Della Street. "Since you're here, better get on the extension phone with your notebook and take notes."

Mason said, "Hello."

The feminine voice which had discussed the matter of a retainer with him earlier in the day sounded eager. "Is this Mr. Mason?"

"Yes."

"Did you get up to court today?"

"Certainly."

"And what did you think?"

"Think of what?"

"Of the case."

"I think probably it will be a hung jury."

"No, no! Of the witness."

"Which witness?"

"The redheaded woman, of course."

"You mean Mrs. Myrtle Anne Haley?"

"Yes."

"I can't tell you."

"You can't tell me?" the voice said, sharp with suspicion. "Why that's what you went up there for. You—"

"I can't discuss my opinion of Mrs. Haley's testimony with a stranger," Mason interrupted firmly.

"A stranger? Why, I'm your client. I—"

"How do I know you're my client?"

"You should be able to recognize my voice."

Mason said, "Voices sound very much alike sometimes. I would dislike very much to have someone claim I had made a libelous statement which wasn't a privileged communication."

There was silence at the other end of the line, then the woman's voice said, "Well, how *could* I identify myself?"

"Through a receipt that I gave the messenger who delivered the hundred dollars to me. When you produce that receipt, I'll know that I'm dealing with the person who made the payment."

"But, Mr. Mason, can't you see? I can't afford to have you know who I am. This whole business of using the messenger was to keep you from finding out."

"Well, I can't give my opinion of testimony unless I'm *certain* my statement is a privileged communication."

"Is your opinion that bad?"

"I am merely enunciating a principle."

"I . . . I already have that receipt, Mr. Mason. The messenger gave it to me."

"Then come on up," Mason said.

There was a long moment of silence.

"I took all these precautions so I wouldn't have to disclose my identity," the voice complained.

"I am taking all these precautions so as to be certain I'm talking to my client," Mason said.

"Will you be there?"

"I'll wait ten minutes. Will that be sufficient?"

"Yes."

"Very well. Come directly to the side door," Mason said.

"I think you're horrid!" she exclaimed. "I didn't want it like this." She slammed the receiver at her end of the telephone.

Mason turned to Della Street, who had been monitoring the conversation. "I take it, Miss Street, that you have decided you're not in a hurry to get home. You'd like to wait."

"Try putting me out of the office," she laughed. "It would take a team of elephants to drag me out."

She took the cover off her typewriter, arranged shorthand notebooks, hung up her hat in the coat closet.

Again the telephone rang.

Mason frowned. "We should have cut out the switchboard as soon as we had our call, Della. Go cut it out now . . . Well, wait a minute. See who's calling."

Della Street picked up the telephone, said, "Hello," then, "Who's calling, please? . . . Where? . . . Well, just a moment. I think he's gone home for the evening. I don't think he's available. I'll see."

She cupped her hand over the mouthpiece of the telephone and said, "A Mr. Guthrie Balfour is calling from Chihuahua City in Mexico. He says it's exceedingly important."

"Balfour?" Mason said. "That will be the uncle of young Ted Balfour, the defendant in this case. Looks like we're getting dragged into a vortex of events, Della. Tell long-distance you've located me and have her put her party on."

Della Street relayed the message into the telephone and a moment later nodded to Mason.

Mason picked up the telephone.

A man's voice at the other end of the line, sounding rather distant and faint, was nevertheless filled with overtones of urgency.

"Is this Perry Mason, the lawyer?"

"That's right," Mason said.

The voice sharpened with excitement. "Mr. Mason, this is Guthrie Balfour. I have just returned from the Tarahumare Indian country and I must get back to my base camp. I've received disquieting news in the mail here at Chihuahua. It seems my nephew, Theodore Balfour, is accused of a hit-and-run death.

"You must know of me, Mr. Mason. I'm quite certain you know of the vast industrial empire of the Balfour Allied Associates. We have investments all over the world—"

"I've heard of you," Mason interrupted. "The case involving your nephew was tried today."

The voice sounded suddenly dispirited and dejected. "What was the verdict?"

"As far as I know, the jury is still out."

"It's too late to do anything now?"

"I think perhaps it will be a hung jury. Why do you ask?"

"Mr. Mason, this is important! This is important as the devil! My nephew *must not* be convicted of anything."

"He can probably get probation in case he's convicted," Mason said. "There are certain facts about the case that make it very peculiar. There are certain discrepancies—"

"Of course there are discrepancies! Can't you understand? The whole thing is a frame-up. It's brought for a specific purpose. Mr. Mason, I can't get away. I'm down here on an archeological expedition of the greatest importance. I'm encountering certain difficulties, certain hazards, but I'm playing for big stakes. I . . . Look, Mr. Mason, I'll tell you what I'll do. I'll put my wife aboard the night plane tonight. She should be able to make connections at El Paso and be in your office the first thing in the morning. What time do you get to your office?"

"Sometime between nine and ten."

"Please, Mr. Mason, give my wife an appointment at nine o'clock in the morning. I'll see that you're amply compensated. I'll see that you—"

32

"The attorney representing your nephew," Mason interrupted, "is Mortimer Dean Howland."

"Howland!" the voice said. "That browbeating, loud-mouthed bag of wind. He's nothing but a medium-grade criminal attorney, with a booming voice. This case is going to take brains, Mr. Mason. This . . . I can't explain. Will you give my wife an appointment for tomorrow morning at nine o'clock?"

"All right," Mason said. "I may not be free to do what you want me to do, however."

"Why?"

"I have some other connections which may bring about a conflict," Mason said. "I can't tell you definitely, but . . . well, anyway, I'll talk with your wife."

"Tomorrow at nine."

"That's right."

"Thank you so much."

Mason hung up. "Well," he said to Della Street, "we seem to be getting deeper and deeper into the frying pan."

"Right in the hot fat," Della observed. "I—" She broke off as a nervous knock sounded on the door of Mason's private office.

Della crossed over and opened the door.

The young woman who had been seated next to Perry Mason in the courtroom entered the office.

"Well, good evening," Mason said. "You weren't very cordial to me earlier in the day."

"Of course not!"

"You wouldn't even give me the time of day."

"I . . . Mr. Mason, you . . . you've jockeyed me into a position . . . well, a position in which I didn't want to be placed."

"That's too bad," the lawyer said. "I was afraid *you* were going to put *me* in a position in which *I* didn't want to be placed."

"Well, you know who I am now."

"Sit down," Mason said. "By the way, just who are you . . . other than Cash?"

"My name is Marilyn Keith, but please don't make any further inquiries."

"Just what is your relationship to Myrtle Anne Haley?"

"Look here, Mr. Mason, you're cross-examining me. That's not what I wanted. I wanted certain information from you. I didn't want you even to know who I am."

"Why?"

"That's neither here nor there."

Mason said, "You're here and it's here. Now what's this all about?"

"I simply *have* to know the real truth—and that gets back to Myrtle Haley's testimony."

"Do you know the man who was killed?"

"No."

"Yet," Mason said, "you have parted with a hundred dollars of your money, money which, I take it, was withdrawn from a rainy-day fund, to retain me to listen to the case in court so you could ask me how I felt about the testimony of Myrtle Anne Haley?"

"That's right. Only the money came from . . . well, it was to have been my vacation fund."

"Vacation?"

"Mine comes next month," she said. "I let the other girls take theirs during the summer. I had intended to go to Acapulco . . . I will, anyway, but . . . well, naturally I hated to draw against my vacation fund. However, that's all in the past now."

"You have the receipt?" Mason asked.

She opened her purse, took from it the receipt which Della Street had given the messenger, and handed it to him.

Mason looked the young woman in the eyes. "I think Myrtle Haley was lying."

For a moment there was a flicker of expression on her face, then she regained her self-control. "Lying deliberately?"

Mason nodded. "Don't repeat my opinion to anyone else.

To you this is a privileged communication. If you repeat what I said to anyone, however, you could get into trouble.''

''Can you . . . can you give me any reasons for your conclusions, Mr. Mason?''

''She wrote down the license number of the automobile,'' Mason said. ''She wrote it down in her notebook in exactly the right place and—''

''Yes, of course. I heard the argument of the defense attorney,'' Marilyn interrupted. ''It sounds logical. But on the other hand, suppose Myrtle *did* take her eyes off the road? That would only have been for a minute. She didn't have her eyes off the road *all* the time she was writing. She just glanced down at the notebook to make certain she had the right place and—''

Mason picked up a pencil and a piece of paper. ''Write down the figure six,'' he instructed Marilyn Keith.

She wrote as he directed.

''Now,'' Mason said, ''get up and walk around the room and write another six while you're walking.''

She followed his instructions.

''Compare the two figures,'' Mason told her.

''I don't see any difference.''

''Bring them over here,'' Mason said, ''and I'll show you some difference.''

She started over toward the desk.

''Wait a minute,'' Mason said. ''Write another figure six while you're walking over here.''

She did so, handed him the pad of paper with the three sixes on it.

''This is the six that you wrote while you were sitting down,'' Mason said. ''You'll notice that the end of the line on the loop of the six comes back and joins the down stroke. Now, look at the two figures that you made while you were walking. In one of them the loop of the six stops approximately a thirty-second of an inch before it comes to the down stroke, and on the second one the end of the loop goes completely through the down stroke and protrudes for probably a thirty-second of an inch on the other side.

"You try to write the figure six when you're riding in an automobile and you'll do one of two things. You'll either stop the end of the loop before you come to the down stroke or you'll go all the way through it. It's only when you're sitting perfectly still that you can bring the end of the six directly to the down stroke and then stop.

"Now, if you'll notice the figure GMB 665 that Myrtle Anne Haley *claims* she wrote while she was in a moving automobile, with one hand on the steering wheel, the other hand holding a fountain pen, writing in a notebook which was balanced on her lap, you'll note that both of the figures are perfect. The loops join the down strokes, so that the loops are perfectly closed. The chances that that could have been done twice in succession by someone who was in a moving automobile, going over the road at a good rate of speed under the circumstances described by Myrtle Anne Haley, are just about one in a million."

"Why didn't the defense attorney bring that out?" she asked.

"Perhaps it didn't occur to him," Mason said. "Perhaps he didn't think he needed to."

She was silent for several seconds, then asked, "Is there anything else?"

"Lots of things," Mason said. "In addition to a sort of sixth sense which warns a lawyer when a witness is lying, there is the question of distance.

"If Mrs. Haley passed that car at the point she says she did, and then looked in the rearview mirror as she says she did, she must have been crossing State Highway when she saw the light go out. She'd hardly have been looking in her rearview mirror while she was crossing State Highway."

"Yes, I can see that," the young woman admitted. "That is, I can see it now that you've pointed it out."

Mason said, "Something caused you to become suspicious of Myrtle Haley's testimony in the first place. Do you want to tell me about it?''

She shook her head. ''I can't.''

''Well,'' Mason said, ''you asked me for my opinion. You paid me a hundred dollars to sit in court and form that opinion. I have now given it to you.''

She thought things over for a moment, then suddenly got up to give him her hand. ''Thank you, Mr. Mason. You're . . . you're everything that I expected.''

''Don't you think you'd better give me your address now?'' Mason said. ''One that we can put on the books?''

''Mr. Mason, I can't! If anyone knew about my having been to you, I'd be ruined. Believe me, there are interests involved that are big and powerful and ruthless. I only hope I haven't gone so far as to get you in trouble.''

Mason studied her anxious features. ''Is there any reason as far as you are concerned why I can't interest myself in any phase of the case?''

''Why do you ask that question?''

''I may have been approached by another potential client.''

She thought that over. ''Surely not Myrtle Haley!''

''No,'' Mason said. ''I would be disqualified as far as she is concerned.''

''Well, who is it?'' she asked.

''I'm not free to tell you that. However, if there is any reason why I shouldn't represent *anyone* who is connected with the case in any way, please tell me.''

She said, ''I would love to know the real truth in this case. If you become connected with it you'll dig out that truth . . . and I don't care who retains you. As far as I'm concerned, you are free to go ahead in any way, Mr. Mason.'' She crossed to the door in one quick movement. ''Good night,'' she said, and closed the door behind her.

Mason turned to Della Street. ''Well?'' he asked.

''She doesn't lie very well,'' Della said.

''Meaning what?''

"She didn't dig into her vacation money just to get your opinion of Myrtle's testimony."

"Then why *did* she do it?"

"I *think*," Della Street said, "she's in love, and I *know* she's frightened."

Chapter 6

Perry Mason latchkeyed the door of his private office, hung up his hat.

Della Street, who was there before him, asked, "Have you seen the morning papers?" She indicated the papers on Mason's desk.

He shook his head.

"There was a hung jury in the case of People versus Ted Balfour. They were divided evenly—six for acquittal and six for conviction."

"So what happened?" Mason asked.

"Apparently, Howland made a deal with the prosecutor. The Court discharged the jury and asked counsel to agree on a new trial date.

"At that time Howland got up, said that he thought the case was costing the state altogether too much money in view of the issues involved. He stated that he would be willing to stipulate the case could be submitted to Judge Cadwell, sitting without a jury, on the same evidence which had been introduced in the jury trial.

"The prosecutor agreed to that. Judge Cadwell promptly announced that under those circumstances he would find the defendant guilty as charged, and Howland thereupon made a motion for suspended sentence. The prosecutor said that under the circumstances and in view of the money that the defendant had saved the state, he would not oppose such a motion, provided the defendant paid a fine. He said he would consent that the matter be heard immediately.

"Judge Cadwell stated that in view of the stipulation by

the prosecutor, he would give the defendant a suspended jail sentence and impose a fine of five hundred dollars.''

"Well, that's interesting," Mason said. "It certainly disposed of the case of People versus Balfour in a hurry. We haven't heard anything from our client of yesterday, have we, Della?"

"No, but our client of today is waiting in the office."

"You mean Mrs. Balfour?"

"That's right."

"How does she impress you, Della? Does she show signs of having been up all night?"

Della Street shook her head. "Fresh as a daisy. Groomed tastefully and expensively. Wearing clothes that didn't come out of a suitcase. She really set out to make an impression on Mr. Perry Mason.

"Apparently she chartered a plane out of Chihuahua, flew to El Paso in time to make connections with one of the luxury planes, arrived home, grabbed a little shut-eye and then this morning started making herself very, very presentable."

"Good-looking?" Mason asked.

"A dish."

"How old?"

"She's in that deadly dangerous age between twenty-seven and thirty-two. That's about as close as I can place her."

"Features?" Mason asked.

"She has," Della Street said, "large brown expressive eyes, a mouth that smiles to show beautiful pearly teeth—in short, she's a regular millionaire's second wife, an expensive plaything. And even so, Mr. Guthrie Balfour must have done a lot of window-shopping before he had this package wrapped up."

"A thoroughly devoted wife," Mason said, smiling.

"Very, very devoted," Della Street said. "Not to Mr. Guthrie Balfour, but to *Mrs.* Guthrie Balfour. There's a woman who's exceedingly loyal to herself."

"Well, get her in," Mason said. "Let's have a look at her.

Now, she's a second wife, so really she's no relation to young Ted Balfour.''

"That's right. You'll think I'm catty," Della Street observed, "but I'll tell you something, Mr. Perry Mason."

"What?"

"You're going to fall for her like a ton of bricks. She's just the type to impress you."

"But not you?" Mason asked.

Della Street's answer was to flash him a single glance.

"Well, bring her in," Mason said, smiling. "After this build-up, I'm bound to be disappointed."

"You won't be," she told him.

Della Street ushered Mrs. Guthrie Balfour into Mason's private office.

Mason arose, bowed, said, "Good morning, Mrs. Balfour. I'm afraid you've had rather a hard trip."

Her smile was radiant. "Not at all, Mr. Mason. In the first place, I was here at home by one-thirty this morning. In the second place, traveling on air-conditioned planes and sitting in sponge rubber reclining seats is the height of luxury compared to the things an archeologist's wife has to contend with."

"Do sit down," Mason said. "Your husband seemed very much disturbed about the case against his nephew."

"That's putting it mildly."

"Well," Mason said, "apparently, the young man's attorney worked out a deal with the prosecutor. Did you read the morning paper?"

"Heavens, no! Was there something in there about the case?"

"Yes," Mason said. "Perhaps you'd like to read it for yourself."

He folded the paper and handed it to her.

While she was reading the paper, Mason studied her carefully.

Suddenly Mrs. Balfour uttered an exclamation of annoyance, crumpled the paper, threw it to the floor, jumped from

41

the chair, and stamped a high-heeled shoe on the paper. Then abruptly she caught herself.

"Oh, I'm sorry," she said. "I didn't realize."

She stepped carefully off the paper, disentangling her high heels, raising her skirts as she did so, so that she disclosed a neat pair of legs. Then, dropping to her knees, she started smoothing the newspaper out.

"I'm so sorry, Mr. Mason," she said contritely. "My temper got the best of me . . . that awful temper of mine."

"Don't bother about the paper," Mason said, glancing at Della Street. "There are plenty more down on the news-stand. Please don't give it another thought."

"No, no . . . I'm sorry. I . . . let me do penance, please, Mr. Mason."

She carefully smoothed out the paper, then arose with supple grace.

"What was there about the article that annoyed you?" Mason asked.

"The fool!" she said. "The absolute fool! Oh, they should never have let that braggart, that loudmouthed egoist handle the case—not for a minute."

"Mortimer Dean Howland?" Mason asked.

"Mortimer Dean Howland," she said, spitting out the words contemptuously. "Look what he's done."

"Apparently," Mason said, "he's made a pretty good deal. In all probability, Mrs. Balfour, while the jury was out, Howland approached the prosecutor, suggested the possibility of a hung jury, and the prosecutor probably didn't care too much about retrying the case. So it was agreed that if there was a hung jury, the case could be submitted to Judge Cadwell on the evidence which had been introduced, which was, of course, equivalent to pleading the defendant guilty, only it saved him the stigma of such a plea.

"The prosecutor, for his side of the bargain, agreed that he would stipulate the judge could pass a suspended sentence and the case would be cleaned up. Of course, the trouble with a stipulation of that sort is that on occasion the judge won't ride along, but takes the bit in his teeth and insists on pronouncing sentence. Judge Cadwell, however, is known for his consideration of the practical problems of the practicing attorney. He virtually always rides along with a stipulation of that sort.''

Mrs. Balfour followed Mason's explanation with intense interest, her large brown eyes showing the extent of her concentration.

When Mason had finished she said simply, ''There are some things that Ted Balfour doesn't know about. Therefore, his attorney could hardly be expected to know them. But they are vital.''

''What, for instance?'' Mason asked.

''Addison Balfour,'' she explained.

''What about him?'' Mason asked.

''He's the wealthiest member of the family, and he's terribly prejudiced.''

''I thought your husband was the wealthy one,'' Mason ventured.

''No. Guthrie is pretty well heeled, I guess. I don't know. I've never inquired into his financial status. Under the circumstances, my motives might have been misunderstood,'' she said, and laughed, a light, nervous laugh.

''Go on,'' Mason said.

''Addison Balfour is dying and knows it. Eighteen months ago the doctors gave him six months to live. Addison is really a remarkable character. He's wealthy, eccentric, strong-minded, obstinate, and completely unpredictable. One thing I do know—if *he* ever learns that Ted Balfour has been convicted of killing a man with an automobile, Addison will disinherit Ted immediately.''

''Ted is mentioned in his will?''

''I have reason to believe so. I think Ted is to receive a large chunk of property, but Addison is very much prejudiced against what he calls the helter-skelter attitude of the younger generation.

''You see, Ted took his military service. He's finished col-

43

lege and is now taking a six-months' breathing spell before he plunges into the business of Balfour Industries.

"Ted had some money which was left him outright by his father. Addison didn't approve of that at all. There is also a fortune left Ted in trust. Ted bought one of these high-powered sports cars that will glide along the highway at one hundred and fifty miles an hour, and Addison had a fit when he learned of that.

"You see, my husband is childless, Addison is childless, and Ted represents the only one who can carry on the Balfour name and the Balfour traditions. Therefore, he's an important member of the family."

"Ted wasn't driving his sports car the night of the accident?" Mason asked.

"No, he was driving one of the big cars."

"There are several?"

"Yes."

"The same make?"

"No. My husband is restless. He's restless mentally as well as physically. Most people will buy one make of car. If they like it, they'll have all their cars of that make. Guthrie is completely different. If he buys a Cadillac today, he'll buy a Buick tomorrow, and an Olds the next day. Then he'll get a Lincoln for his next car, and so on down the line. I've only been married to him for two years, but I guess I've driven half a dozen makes of cars in that time."

"I see," Mason said. "Now, just what did you have in mind?"

"In the first place," she said, "this man Howland must go. Do you have any idea how it happened that Ted went to him in the first place?"

Mason shook his head.

"You see, my husband and I left for Mexico the day of the accident. This happened the night we left. Ted was very careful that we didn't hear anything about it. We've been back in the wild barranca country. We came to Chihuahua for mail and supplies and there was a letter there from the trustee of

44

Ted's trust fund. Guthrie called you immediately after he'd read that letter. He simply had to return to base camp, and from there he's going out on a very dangerous but exciting expedition into very primitive country."

"You went by train?"

"Yes. My husband doesn't like airplanes. He says they're nothing but buses with wings. He likes to get in an air-conditioned train, get single occupancy of a drawing room, stretch out, relax and do his thinking. He says he does some of his best thinking and nearly all of his best sleeping on a train."

"Well," Mason said, "the case has been concluded. There's nothing for me or anyone else to do now."

"That's not the way my husband feels about it. Despite the court's decision, he'll want you to check on the evidence of the witnesses."

"What good would that do?"

"You could get the stipulation set aside and get a new trial."

"That would be difficult."

"Couldn't you do it if you could prove one of the main witnesses was lying?"

"Perhaps. Do you think one of the main witnesses was lying?"

"I'd want to have you investigate that and tell me."

"I couldn't do anything as long as Howland was representing Ted."

"He's finished now."

"Does he know that?"

"He will."

Mason said, "There's one other matter you should know about."

"What?"

"Without discussing details," Mason said, "I was retained to sit in court yesterday and listen to the evidence in the case."

"By whom?"

"I am not at liberty to disclose that. I'm not certain I know."

"But for heaven's sake, why should anyone ask you simply to sit in court and listen?"

"That," Mason said, "is something I've been asking myself. The point is that I *did* it. Now I don't want to have any misunderstandings about this. I have had one client who asked me to sit in court and listen."

"And you sat in court and listened?"

"Yes."

"What did you think of the case?"

"There again," Mason said, "is something I have to discuss cautiously. I came to the conclusion that one of the principal witnesses might not be telling the truth."

"A witness for the prosecution?"

"Yes. The defense put on no case."

"Well, is that going to disqualify you from doing what we want?"

"Not unless you think it does. It complicates the situation in that Howland will think I deliberately watched the trial in order to steal his client."

"Do you care what Howland thinks?"

"In a way, yes."

"But it's not going to be too important?"

"Not *too* important. I would like to have the matter adjusted so that Howland can understand the situation."

"You leave Howland to me," she said. "I'm going to talk with him, and when I get done telling him a few things, he'll know how my husband and I feel."

"After all," Mason said, "Ted is apparently the one who retained him, and Ted is over twenty-one and able to do as he pleases."

"Well, I am going to talk with Ted, too."

"Do so," Mason said. "Get in touch with me after you have clarified the situation. I don't want to touch it while Howland is in the picture."

Mrs. Balfour whipped out a checkbook. "You are retained as of right now," she said.

She took a fountain pen, wrote out a check for a thousand dollars, signed it *Guthrie Balfour, per Dorla Balfour*, and handed it to Mason.

"I don't get it," the lawyer said. "Here's a case that's all tried and finished and now you come along with a retainer."

"Your work will lie in convincing Addison that Ted wasn't really involved in that case," she said. "And there'll be plenty of work and responsibility, don't think there won't be.

"For one thing, you're going to have to reopen the case. Frankly, Mr. Mason, while Addison may blame Ted, he'll be furious at Guthrie for letting any such situation develop. He thinks Guthrie puts in too much time on these expeditions.

"Just wait until you see what you're up against, and you'll understand what I mean.

"And now I must go see Ted, let Howland know he's fired and . . . well, I'm going to let *you* deal with Addison. When you see him, remember *we've* retained you to protect Ted's interests.

"Will you hold some time open for me later on today?" she asked.

Mason nodded.

"You'll hear from me," she promised and walked out.

When the door had clicked shut, Mason turned to Della Street. "Well?"

Della Street motioned toward the crumpled newspaper. "An impulsive woman," she said.

"A very interesting woman," Mason said. "She's using her mind all the time. Did you notice the way she was concentrating when I was explaining what had happened in the case?"

"I noticed the way she was looking at you while you were talking," Della Street said.

"Her face was the picture of concentration. She is using her head all the time."

"I also noticed the way she walked out the door," Della Street said. "She may have been using her mind when she was looking at you, but she was using her hips when she knew you were looking at her."

Mason said, "You were also looking."

"Oh, she *knew* I'd be looking," Della Street said, "but the act was strictly for your benefit."

Chapter 7

It was ten-thirty when Mason's unlisted phone rang. Since only Della Street and Paul Drake, head of the Drake Detective Agency, had the number of that telephone, Mason reached across the desk for it. "I'll answer it," he said to Della, and then, picking up the receiver, said, "Hello, Paul."

Paul Drake's voice came over the wire with the toneless efficiency of an announcer giving statistical reports on an election night.

"You're interested in the Ted Balfour case, Perry," he said. "There have been some developments in that case you ought to know about."

"In the first place, how did you know I am interested?" Mason asked.

"You were in court yesterday following the case."

"Who told you?"

"I get around," Drake said. "Listen. There's something funny in that case. It may have been a complete frame-up."

"Yes?" Mason asked. "What makes you think so?"

"The body's been identified," Drake said.

"And what does that have to do with it?" Mason asked.

"Quite a good deal."

"Give me the dope. Who is the man?"

"A fellow by the name of Jackson Eagan. At least that's the name he gave when he registered at the Sleepy Hollow Motel. It's also the name he gave when he rented a car from a drive-yourself agency earlier that day."

"Go on," Mason said.

"The people who rented the car made a recovery of the car within a day or two. It had been left standing in front of

49

the motel. The management reported it; the car people assumed it was just one of those things that happen every so often when a man signs up for a car, then changes his mind about something and simply goes away without notifying the agency. Since the car people had a deposit of fifty dollars, they simply deducted rental for three days, set the balance in a credit fund, and said nothing about it. Therefore, the police didn't know that Jackson Eagan was missing. The motel people didn't care because Eagan had paid his rent in advance. So if it hadn't been for a fluke, the police would never have discovered the identity of the body. The features were pretty well damaged, you remember."

"What was the fluke?" Mason asked.

"When the body was found there was nothing in the pockets except some odds and ends that offered no chance for an identification, some small coins and one key. The police didn't pay much attention to the key until someone in the police department happened to notice a code number on the key. This man was in the traffic squad and he said the code number was that of a car rental agency. So the police investigated, and sure enough, this key was for the car that had been parked in front of the motel for a couple of days."

"When did they find out all this?" Mason asked.

"Yesterday morning, while the case was being tried. They didn't get the dope to the prosecutor until after the arguments had started, but police knew about it as early as eight o'clock. The reason it didn't reach the prosecutor was on account of red tape in the D.A.'s office. The guy who handles that stuff decided it wouldn't make any difference in the trial, so he let it ride."

"That's most interesting," Mason said. "It may account for the sudden desire on the part of a lot of people to retain my services."

"Okay. I thought you'd be interested," Drake said.

"Keep an ear to the ground, Paul," Mason said, hung up the telephone and repeated the conversation to Della Street.

"Where does that leave you, Chief?" she asked.

"Where I always am," Mason said, "right in the middle. There's something phony about this whole business. That Haley woman was reciting a whole synthetic lie there on the witness stand, and people don't lie like that unless there's a reason."

"And," Della Street said, "young women like Marilyn Keith don't give up their vacation to Acapulco unless there's a reason."

"Nor women like Mrs. Guthrie Balfour literally force retainers on reluctant attorneys," Mason said. "Stick around, Della. I think you'll see some action."

Della Street smiled sweetly at her employer. "I'm sticking," she announced simply.

Chapter 8

By one forty-five Mrs. Balfour was back in Mason's office.

"I've seen Ted," she said.

Mason nodded.

"It's just as I surmised. Ted was given a loaded drink. He passed out. I don't know who had it in for him or why, but I can tell you one thing."

"What?"

"He wasn't the one who was driving his car," she asserted. "A young woman drove him home—a cute trick with dark chestnut hair, a nice figure, good legs, and a very sympathetic shoulder. I think I can find out who she was by checking the list of party guests. It was a party given by Florence Ingle."

"How do you know about the girl?" Mason asked.

"A friend of mine saw her driving Ted's car, with Ted passed out and leaning on her shoulder. He'd seen her at the parking space getting into Ted's car. She had Ted move over and she took the wheel. If anyone hit a pedestrian with the car Ted had that evening, it was that girl."

"At what time was this?" Mason asked.

"Sometime between ten and eleven."

"And after Ted got home what happened?" Mason asked.

"Now as to that," she said, "you'll have to find the young woman who was driving and ask her. There were no servants in the house. Remember, Guthrie and I had taken the train. Before that there'd been a farewell party at Florence Ingle's. I'd told all of our servants to take the night off. There was no one at our house."

"Ted was in his bedroom the next morning?" Mason asked.

"Apparently he was. He told me he became conscious at four thirty-five in the morning. Someone had taken him upstairs, undressed him, and put him to bed."

"Or he undressed himself and put himself to bed," Mason said.

"He was in no condition to do that."

"Any idea who this girl was?" Mason asked.

"Not yet. Ted either doesn't know or won't tell. Apparently, she was some trollop from the wrong side of the tracks."

Mason's frown showed annoyance.

"All right, all right," she said. "I'm out of order. I'm not a snob. Remember, Mr. Mason, I came from the wrong side of the tracks myself, and I made it, but I'm just telling you it's a long, hard climb. And also remember, Mr. Mason, you're working for me."

"The hell I am," Mason said. "You're paying the bill, but I'm working for my client."

"Now don't get stuffy," she said, flashing her teeth in a mollifying smile. "I had Ted write a check covering Howland's fees in full and I explained to Mr. Howland that as far as Mr. Guthrie Balfour and I were concerned, we preferred to have all further legal matters in connection with the case handled by Mr. Perry Mason."

"And what did Howland say then?"

"Howland threw back his head, laughed and said, 'If it's a fair question, Mrs. Balfour, when did you get back from Mexico?' and I told him that I didn't know whether it was a fair question or not, but there was no secret about it and I got back from Mexico on a plane which arrived half an hour past midnight, and then he laughed again and said that if I had arrived twenty-four hours sooner he felt certain he wouldn't have had the opportunity to represent Ted as long as he did."

"He was a little put out about it?" Mason asked.

"On the contrary, he was in rare good humor. He said that he had completed his representation of Ted Balfour, that the case was closed, and that if Mr. Mason knew as much about the case as he did, Mason would realize the over-all strategy had been brilliant."

"Did he say in what respect?"

"No, but he gave me a letter for you."

"Indeed," Mason said.

She unfolded the letter and extended it across the desk. The letter was addressed to Perry Mason and read:

MY DEAR COUNSELOR,

I now begin to see a great light. I trust your time in court was well spent, but don't worry. There are no hard feelings. You take on from here and more power to you. I consider myself completely relieved of all responsibilities in the case of the People versus Ted Balfour, and I am satisfied, not only with the compensation I have received, but with the outcome of my strategy. From here on, the Balfour family is all yours. They consider me a little crude and I consider them highly unappreciative in all ways except insofar as financial appreciation is concerned. I can assure you that those matters have been completely taken care of, so consider yourself free to gild the lily or paint the rose in any way you may see fit, remembering only that it's advisable to take the temperature of the water before you start rocking the boat.

With all good wishes,
MORTIMER DEAN HOWLAND

"A very interesting letter," Mason said, handing it to Mrs. Balfour.

"Isn't it?" she remarked dryly after having read it. She returned it to Perry Mason.

"*Now*, what do you want me to do?" Mason asked.

"The first thing I want you to do," she said, "is to go and

see Addison Balfour. He's in bed. He'll never get out of bed. You'll have to go to him.''

"Will he see me?"

"He'll see you. I've already telephoned for an appointment.''

"When?" Mason asked.

"I telephoned about thirty minutes ago. The hour of the appointment, however, is to be left to you. Mr. Addison Balfour will be *very* happy to see the great Perry Mason.''

Mason turned to Della Street. "Ring up Addison Balfour's secretary,'' he said, "and see if I can have an appointment for three o'clock.''

Chapter 9

Some two years earlier, when the doctors had told Addison Balfour that he had better "take it easy for a while," the manufacturing magnate had moved his private office into his residence.

Later on, when the doctors had told him frankly that he had but six months to live at the outside, Addison Balfour had moved his office into his bedroom.

Despite the sentence of death which had been pronounced upon him, he continued to be the same old irascible, unpredictable fighter. Disease had ravaged his body, but the belligerency of the man's mind remained unimpaired.

Mason gave his name to the servant who answered the door.

"Oh, yes, Mr. Mason. You are to go right up. Mr. Balfour is expecting you. The stairs to the left, please."

Mason climbed the wide flight of oak stairs, walked down the second floor toward a sign which said "Office," and entered through an open door, from behind which came the sound of pounding typewriters.

Two stenographers were busily engaged in hammering keyboards. A telephone operator sat at the back of a room, supervising a switchboard.

At a desk facing the door sat Marilyn Keith.

"Good afternoon," Mason said calmly and impersonally as though he had never before seen her. "I am Mr. Mason. I have an appointment with Mr. Addison Balfour."

"Just a moment, Mr. Mason. I'll tell Mr. Balfour you're here."

She glided from the room through an open doorway and in a moment returned.

"Mr. Balfour will see you now, Mr. Mason," she said in the manner of one reciting a prepared speech which had been repeated so many times and under such circumstances that the repetition had made the words almost without meaning. "You will understand, Mr. Mason, that Mr. Addison Balfour is not at all well. He is, for the moment, confined to his bed. Mr. Balfour dislikes to discuss his illness with anyone. You will, therefore, please try to act as though the situation were entirely normal and you were seeing Mr. Balfour in his office. However, you will remember he is ill and try to conclude the interview as soon as possible.

"You may go in now."

She ushered Mason through the open door, along a vestibule, then swung open a heavy oaken door which moved on well-oiled hinges.

The man who was propped up in bed might have been made of colorless wax. His high cheekbones, the gaunt face, the sunken eyes, all bore the unmistakable stamp of illness. But the set of his jaw, the thin, determined line of his mouth showed the spirit of an indomitable fighter.

Balfour's voice was not strong. "Come in, Mr. Mason," he said in a monotone, as though he lacked the physical strength to put even the faintest expression in his words. "Sit down here by the bed. What's all this about Ted getting convicted?"

Mason said, "The attorney who was representing your nephew appeared to think that the interests of expediency would best be served by making a deal with the district attorney's office."

"Who the hell wants to serve the interests of expediency?" Balfour asked in his colorless, expressionless voice.

"Apparently your nephew's attorney thought that would be best under the circumstances."

"What do you think?"

"I don't know."

"Find out."

"I intend to."

"Come back when you find out."

"Very well," Mason said, getting up.

"Wait a minute. Don't go yet. *I* want to tell *you* something. Lean closer. Listen. Don't interrupt."

Mason leaned forward so that his ear was but a few inches from the thin, colorless lips.

"I told Dorla—that's Guthrie's wife—that I'd disinherit Ted if he got in any trouble with that automobile. That was just a bluff.

"Ted's a Balfour. He has the Balfour name. He's going to carry it on. It would be unthinkable to have the Balfour Allied Associates carried on by anyone who wasn't a Balfour. I want Ted to marry. I want him to have children. I want him to leave the business to a man-child who has the name of Balfour and the characteristics of a Balfour. Do you understand?"

Mason nodded.

"But," Addison went on, "I want to be sure that Ted knows the duties and responsibilities of a Balfour and of the head of a damn big business."

Again Mason nodded.

Addison Balfour waited for a few seconds as though mustering his strength.

Addison Balfour breathed deeply, exhaled in a tremulous sigh, took in his breath once more and said, "Balfours don't compromise, Mr. Mason. Balfours fight."

Mason waited.

"Lots of times you win a case by a compromise," Balfour said. "It's a good thing. You may come out better in some isolated matter by compromise than by fighting a thing through to the last bitter ditch.

"That's a damn poor way to go through life.

"Once people know that you'll compromise when the going gets tough, they see to it that the going gets tough. People aren't dumb. Businessmen get to know the caliber of the

58

businessmen they are dealing with. Balfours don't compromise.

"We won't fight unless we're in the right. When we start fighting, we carry the fight through to the end.

"You understand what I mean, Mason?"

Mason nodded.

"We don't want the reputation of being compromisers," Balfour continued. "We want the reputation of being implacable fighters. I want Ted to learn that lesson.

"I'd told Guthrie's wife that I'd disinherit Ted if he ever got convicted of any serious accident with that automobile. Scared her to death. She has her eye out for the cash. What do you think of her, Mason?"

"I'm hardly in a position to discuss her," Mason said.

"Why not?"

"She's somewhat in the position of a client."

"The hell she is! Ted Balfour is your client. What makes you say she's a client? She didn't retain you, did she?"

"For Ted Balfour."

"She did that because Guthrie told her to. How was the check signed?"

"Your brother's name, Guthrie Balfour, per Dorla Balfour."

"That's what I thought. She wouldn't give you a thin dime out of her money. Heaven knows how much she's got! She's milked Guthrie for plenty. That's all right. That's Guthrie's business.

"Don't be misled about money, Mason. You can't eat money. You can't wear money. All you can do with money is spend it. That's what it's for.

"Guthrie wanted a good-looker. He had money. He bought one. The trouble is, people aren't merchandise. You can pay for them, but that doesn't mean you've got 'em. Personally, I wouldn't trust that woman as far as I could throw this bed, and that isn't very damn far, Mason. Do you understand me?"

"I understand the point you're making."

"Remember it!" Balfour said. "Now, I want young Ted to fight. I don't want him to start out by compromising. When I read the paper this morning I was furious. I was going to send for you myself, but Dorla telephoned my secretary and told her she'd made arrangements to have you step into the picture. What are you going to do, Mason?"

"I don't know."

"Get in there and fight like hell! Don't worry about money. You have a retainer?"

"A retainer," Mason said, "which at first blush seemed more than adequate."

"How does it seem now?"

"Adequate."

"Something happened?"

"The case has taken on certain unusual aspects."

"All right," Balfour said. "You're in the saddle. Start riding the horse. Pick up the reins. Don't let anybody tell you what to do. You're not like most of these criminal lawyers. You don't want just to get a client off. You try to dig out the truth. I like that. That's what I want.

"Now remember this: If a Balfour is wrong, he apologizes and makes restitution. If he's right, he fights. Now you start fighting.

"I don't want you to tell Dorla that I'm not going to disinherit Ted. I don't want you to tell Ted. I want Ted to sweat a little blood. Ted's going to have to get in the business pretty quick, and he's going to have to become a Balfour. He isn't a Balfour now. He's just a kid. He's young. He's inexperienced. He hasn't been tempered by fire.

"This experience is going to do him good. It's going to teach him that he has to fight. It's going to teach him that he can't go through life playing around on his dad's money. Scare the hell out of him if you want to, but make him fight.

"Now I'll tell you one other thing, Mason. Don't trust Dorla."

Mason remained silent.

"Well?" Addison Balfour snapped.

60

"I heard you," Mason said.

"All right, I'm telling you. Don't trust Dorla. Dorla's a snob. Ever notice how it happens that people who have real background and breeding are considerate, tolerant, and broad-minded, while people who haven't anything except money that they didn't earn themselves are intolerant? That's Dorla. She's got about the nicest figure I've ever seen on a woman. And I've seen lots of them.

"Don't underestimate her, Mason. She's smart. She's chain lightning! She's got her eye on a big slice of money, and Guthrie hasn't waked up yet. That's all right. Let him sleep. He's paid for a dream. As long as he's enjoying the dream, why grab him by the shoulder and bring him back to the grim realities of existence?

"Guthrie isn't really married to Dorla. He's married to the woman he visualizes beneath Dorla's beautiful exterior. It's not the real woman. It's a dream woman, a sort of man-made spouse that he's conjured up out of his own mind.

"When Guthrie wakes up he'll marry Florence Ingle and really be happy. Right now he's a sleepwalker. He's in a dream. Don't try to wake him up.

"I'm a dying man. I can't bring up Ted. After Ted's family died Guthrie and his wife took over. Then Guthrie's wife died and he bought beauty on the auction block. He thought that was what he wanted.

"He knows I'll raise hell if he neglects Ted's bringing up. Dorla isn't a good influence on Ted. She isn't a good influence on anyone. But she's smart! Damned smart!

"If she has to get out from under, she'll trap you to save her own skin. Don't think she can't do it.

"Guthrie gave you a retainer. Don't bother about sending him bills. Send bills to the Balfour Allied Associates. I'll instruct the treasurer to let you have any amount you need. I know you by reputation well enough to know you won't stick me. You should know me by reputation well enough to know that if you overcharge me it'll be the biggest mistake you ever made in your life. That's all now, Mason. I'm going to sleep. Tell my secretary not to disturb me for thirty minutes, no matter what happens. Don't try to shake hands. I get tired. Close the door when you go out. Good-by.''

Addison's head dropped back against the pillow. The colorless eyelids fluttered shut over the faded blue eyes.

Mason tiptoed from the room.

Marilyn Keith was waiting for him on the other side of the vestibule door. ''Will you step this way, please, Mr. Mason?''

Mason followed her into another office and gave her Balfour's message. Marilyn indicated a telephone and a desk. ''We have strict instructions not to put through any phone messages to anyone who is in conference with Mr. Balfour,'' she said. ''But Miss Street telephoned and said you must call at once upon a matter of the greatest urgency.''

''Did she leave any other message?'' Mason asked.

Marilyn Keith shook her head.

Mason dialed the number of the unlisted telephone in his office.

When he heard Della Street's voice on the line he said, ''Okay, Della, what cooks?''

''Paul's here,'' she said. ''He wants to talk with you. Are you where you can talk?''

''Fairly well,'' Mason said.

''Alone?''

''No.''

''Better be careful about what comments you make, then,'' she said. ''Here's Paul. I'll explain to him that you'll have to be rather guarded.''

A moment later Paul Drake's voice came on the line. ''Hello, Perry.''

''Hi,'' Mason said, without mentioning Drake's name.

''Things are happening fast in that Balfour case.''

''What?''

''They secured an order for the exhumation of the corpse.''

''Go ahead.''

''That was done secretly at an early hour this morning.''

62

"Keep talking."

"When police checked at the motel, back-tracking the car, they learned something that started them really moving in a hurry. Apparently someone in the motel had heard a shot on the night of the nineteenth. They dug the body up. The coroner opened the skull, something which had never been done before."

"It hadn't?"

"No. The head had been pretty well smashed up and the coroner evidently didn't go into it."

"Okay, what happened?"

"When they opened the head," Paul Drake said, "they found that it wasn't a hit-and-run accident at all."

"What do you mean?"

"The man had been killed," Drake said, "by a small-caliber, high-powered bullet."

"They're certain?"

"Hell, yes! The bullet's still in there. The hole was concealed beneath the hair and the coroner missed it the first time. Of course, Perry, they thought they were dealing with a hit-and-run death and that the victim was a drifter who had been walking along the road. The whole thing indicated a ne'er-do-well who happened to get in front of a car being driven by an intoxicated driver."

"And now?"

"Hell's bells!" Paul Drake said. "Do I have to draw you a diagram? Now it's first-degree murder."

"Okay," Mason said. "Start working."

"What do you want, Perry?"

"Everything," Mason said. "I'll discuss it with you when I see you. In the meantime, get started."

"What's the limit?" Drake asked.

"There isn't any."

"Okay, I'm starting."

Mason hung up and turned to Marilyn Keith. "Well?" he asked.

"Have you told anyone about me?"

"Not by name."

"Don't."

"I'm in the case now."

"I know."

"It may be more of a case than it seemed at first."

"I know."

"I'm representing Ted."

"Yes, of course."

"You know what that means?"

"What?"

"I may have to show who was really driving the car."

She thought that over for a minute, then raised her chin. "Go right ahead, Mr. Mason. You do anything that will help Ted."

"This case may have a lot more to it than you think," Mason told her. "Do you want to tell me anything?"

"I drove the car," she said.

"Was that the reason you came to me?"

"No."

"Why?"

"On account of Ted. Oh, please, Mr. Mason, don't let anything happen to him. I don't only mean about the car; I mean—lots of things."

"Such as what?" Mason asked.

"Ted's being exposed to influences that aren't good."

"Why aren't they good?"

"I can't tell you all of it," she said. "Mr. Addison Balfour is a wonderful man, but he's an old man. He's a sick man. He's a grim man. He looks at life as a battle. He was never married. He regrets that fact now, not because he realizes that he missed a lot of love, but only because he has no son to carry on the Balfour business.

"He wants to make Ted a second Addison Balfour. He wants to make him a grim, uncompromising, unyielding fighter.

"Ted's young. His vision, his ideals are younger and clearer than those of Addison Balfour. He sees the beauties of life. He can enjoy a sunset or the soft spring sunlight on green hills. He sees and loves beauty everywhere. It would be a tragic mistake to make him into a grim, fighting machine like Addison Balfour.''

"Any other influences?" Mason asked.

"Yes."

"What?"

"The influence of beauty," she said.

"I thought you said you wanted him to appreciate beauty."

"Real beauty, not the spurious kind."

"Who's the spurious beauty?" Mason asked.

"Dorla."

"You mean to say she's married to his uncle and has her eyes on the nephew?"

"She has big eyes," Marilyn Keith said. "Oh, Mr. Mason, I *do* so hope you can handle this thing in such a way that . . . well, give Ted an opportunity to develop his own individuality in his own way. There'll be lots of time later on for him to become as grim as Addison Balfour, and a lot of time later on for him to become disillusioned about women.

"And if Guthrie Balfour should think that Ted and Dorla . . . Mr. Mason, you're a lawyer. You know the world."

"What you have outlined," Mason said, "or rather, what you have hinted at, sounds like quite a combination."

"That," she said, "is a masterpiece of understatement. You haven't met Banner Boles yet."

"Who's he?"

"He's the trouble shooter for the Balfour interests. He's deadly and clever, and whenever he's called in he starts manipulating facts and twisting things around so you don't know where you're at. Oh, Mr. Mason, I'm terribly afraid!"

"For yourself?"

"No, for Ted."

"You may not be in the clear on this thing," Mason said, his voice kindly, "and now that I'm representing Ted, I may have to drag you in."

"Drag me in if it will help Ted."

"Does he know you drove him home?"

"He's never intimated it if he does."

"What happened?"

"He was out in the parking space back of Florence Ingle's place. He wasn't drunk. He was sick. I knew he couldn't drive in that condition. I saw him trying to back up the car. He was barely able to sit up."

"Did you speak to him?"

"I just said, 'Move over,' and I got behind the steering wheel and drove him home."

"What happened?"

"The last part of that trip he was falling over against me, and I'd have to push his weight away so I could drive the car. He'd fall against the wheel. I guess I was going all over the road there on Sycamore Road, but I didn't hit anyone, Mr. Mason. That is, I don't *think* I did. I kept my eyes on the road. I tried to, but he would lurch against me and grab the wheel. I should have stopped, but I wasn't driving fast."

"You put him to bed?"

"I had a terrible time. I finally got him to stagger up to his room. I took his shoes off. I tried to find a servant, but there didn't seem to be anyone at home."

"What time was this?"

"A lot earlier than Myrtle Haley said it was."

Mason was thoughtful. "How did you get home? If you called a cab we may be able to find the driver and establish a time element by—"

"I didn't call a cab, Mr. Mason. I was afraid that might be embarrassing to Ted—a young woman leaving the house alone, the servants all away. I walked to the highway and thumbed a ride. I told the man who picked me up a story of having to walk home."

Mason looked at her sharply.

"There was no reason why any young woman couldn't have called a cab from that house at ten-thirty or eleven at night."

"Don't you see?" she pleaded. "I'm not just any young woman. I'm Addison Balfour's confidential secretary. I know the contents of his will. If he thought I had any interest in Ted . . . or that I had been in Ted's room— Oh, Mr. Mason, please have confidence in me and *please* protect my secret!

"I have to go now. I don't want the girls in the office to get suspicious. I'm supposed to be letting you use the phone. The switchboard operator will know how long it's been since you hung up. Good-by now."

Mason left Addison Balfour's residence, stopped at the first telephone booth, called Paul Drake, said, "I can talk now, Paul. Here's your first job. Find out where Ted Balfour is. Get him out of circulation. Keep him out of circulation. Get in touch with me as soon as you have him and—"

"Whoa, whoa," Drake said. "Back up. You're not playing tiddlywinks. This is for high stakes, and it's for keeps."

"What do you mean?" Mason asked.

"Hell!" Drake said. "The police had Ted in custody within fifteen minutes of the time the autopsy surgeon picked up the telephone and made his first preliminary report about the bullet."

"Where are they keeping him?" Mason asked.

"That's something no one knows," Drake said.

"How about the press, Paul?"

"Figure it out for yourself, Perry. Here's the only heir to the to the Balfour fortune charged with a murder rap which was dressed up to look like a hit-and-run accident. What would you do if you were a city editor?"

"Okay," Mason said wearily. "Get your men working. I'm on my way to the office."

Chapter 10

Mason hurried to his office and started mapping out a plan of campaign before he had even hung up his hat.

"Paul," he said to the detective, "I want to find out everything I can about Jackson Eagan."

"Who doesn't?" Drake said. "If they'd been on the job, police would have spotted this as a murder right at the start. I've seen photographs of the body, Perry. You don't smash up a man's head like that in a hit and run. That man had been tied to a car somehow and his face had literally been dragged over the road. His head was then smashed in with a sledge hammer or something. It was done so the authorities would never think to look for a bullet.

"It worked, too. They thought the guy had been hit, his head dashed to the pavement and then his clothes had caught on the front bumper and he'd been dragged for a while."

"Couldn't it have been that way?" Mason asked.

"Not with the bullet in the guy's brain," Drake said.

"All right," Mason told him, "let's use our heads. The police are concentrating on Ted Balfour. They're trying to get admissions from him. They're trying to check what he was doing on the night of the nineteenth of September. They'll be putting all sorts of pressure on him to make him disclose the identity of the girl whom he remembers as having driven the car.

"There's just a chance that by using our heads we may have just a few minutes' head start on the police on some of these other angles that they won't think of at the moment.

"Now, these car rental agencies won't rent a car unless they see a driver's license, and they usually make a note on the contract of the number of the driver's license. Have operatives cover the car rental agency, take a look at the contract covering the Jackson Eagan car on that date. See if we can get the number of the driver's license from the contract.

"There's a chance we can beat the police to it in another direction. The police won't be able to get in the Balfour house until they get a search warrant or permission from Ted Balfour. Quite frequently you can tell a lot by going through a man's room. They'll be searching his clothes for bloodstains. They'll be looking for a revolver. They'll be doing all of the usual things within a matter of minutes, if they aren't doing it already.

"Della, get Mrs. Guthrie Balfour on the phone for me. Paul, get your men started covering all these other angles."

Drake nodded, said, "I'll go down to my office, so I won't be tying up your telephone system, Perry. I'll have men on the job within a matter of seconds."

"Get going," Mason said.

In the meantime, Della Street's busy fingers had been whirring the dial of the unlisted telephone which was used in times of emergency to get quick connections. A moment later she nodded to Perry Mason and said, "I have Mrs. Balfour on the line."

Mason's voice showed relief. "That's a break," he said. "I was afraid she might be out."

Mason picked up the telephone, said, "Hello, Mrs. Balfour."

"Yes, Mr. Mason, what is it?"

"There have been some very important and very disturbing developments in the matter which you discussed with me."

"There have?" she asked, apprehension in her voice.

"That's right."

"You mean . . . you mean that the matter has been—Why I thought—"

"It doesn't have anything to do with that matter, but a

development from it," Mason said. "The police are now investigating a murder."

"A murder!"

"That's right. I don't want to discuss it on the phone."

"How can I see you?"

Mason said, "Wait there. Don't go out under any circumstances. I'm coming over as soon as I can get there."

Mason slammed up the telephone, said to Della Street, "Come on, Della. Bring a notebook and some pencils. Let's go!"

Mason's long legs striding rapidly down the corridor forced Della Street into a half run in order to keep up. They descended in the elevator, hurried over to Mason's car in the parking lot, and swung into traffic.

"Do you know the way?" Della Street asked.

"Fortunately I do," Mason said. "We go out the State Highway. The scene of the accident was only about a mile from the Balfour estate, and maps were introduced in the case yesterday. You see, the prosecution was trying to prove that Ted Balfour would normally have used this route along Sycamore Road to the State Highway, then turned up State Highway until he came to the next intersection, which would have been the best way to the Balfour estate."

"If there was a murder," Della Street said, "how can they prove that Ted Balfour was in on it?"

"That's what they're *trying* to do right now," Mason said. "They have a pretty good case of circumstantial evidence, indicating that Balfour's *car* was mixed up in it, but they can't prove Balfour was mixed up in it, at least, not from any evidence they had yesterday."

"So what happens?"

"So," Mason said, "*we* try to find and appraise evidence before the police think to look for it."

"Isn't it illegal to tamper with evidence in a case of this sort?"

"We're not going to tamper with evidence," Mason said. "We're going to *look* at it. Once the police get hold of it,

70

they'll put it away and we won't be able to find out anything until we get to court. But if we get a look at it first, we'll know generally what we're up against."

"You think some evidence may be out there?" Della Street asked.

"I don't know," Mason told her. "I hope not. Let's look at it this way, Della: the man was shot. The body was mutilated to conceal the gunshot wound and prevent identification. Then it was taken out and placed by the side of the road. They waited for the tipsy driver to come along and then they threw the body out in front of the car."

"Why do you say 'they'?" Della Street asked.

"Because one man wouldn't be juggling a body around like that."

"Then Ted Balfour may have simply been the means to an end?"

"Exactly."

"But how did they know that a tipsy driver *would* be coming along that road?"

"That's the point," Mason said. "Somebody loaded Balfour's drink. He probably wasn't only intoxicated; he was doped."

"Then how do you account for his testimony that a girl was driving the car?" Della Street asked.

"That was probably a coincidence. It *may* not be the truth."

"That was Ted's story," Della Street said.

"Exactly. Myrtle Anne Haley swore that she was following a car that was weaving all over the road. The prosecutor didn't ask her who was driving the car, whether it was a man or a woman, whether there was one person in the driver's seat, or whether there were two."

"And all those head injuries," Della Street asked, "were simply for the purpose of preventing the corpse from being identified?"

"Probably for the primary purpose of concealing the fact that there was a bullet hole in the head."

"Would Ted Balfour have been mixed up in anything like that?"

"He could have been. We don't know. We don't know the true situation. Myrtle Haley is lying at least about some things. But that doesn't mean *all* of her testimony is false. I think she wrote down that license number sometime after she got home. I think she wrote it down in good light and while she was seated at a table. But her testimony may well be true that she was following a car which was weaving all over the road."

"Then Ted must have been driving it?"

"Don't overlook one other possibility," Mason said. "Ted may have been sent home and put to bed in an intoxicated condition, and then someone took the automobile out of the garage, started weaving all over the road as though driving in an intoxicated condition, waited until he was certain some car behind him would spot him and probably get the license number, then the dead body of Jackson Eagan was thrown in front of the automobile."

"But why?" Della Street asked.

"That," Mason said, "is what we're going to try to find out."

On two occasions after that Della Street started to say something, but each time, glancing up at the lawyer's face, she saw the expression of extreme concentration which she knew so well, and remained silent.

Mason slowed at the intersection, turned from State Highway, ran for about two hundred yards over a surfaced road, and turned to the right between huge stone pillars marking the driveway entrance in a stucco wall which enclosed the front part of the Balfour estate.

The tires crunched along the graveled driveway, and almost as soon as Mason had brought his car to a stop, the front door was thrown open by Mrs. Guthrie Balfour.

Mason, followed by Della Street, hurried up the steps.

"What is it?" she asked.

"Have the police been here yet?" Mason asked.

"Heavens, no!"

"They're coming," Mason said. "We're fighting minutes. Let's take a look in Ted's room."

"But why, Mr. Mason?"

"Do you know a Jackson Eagan?"

"Jackson Eagan," she repeated. "No, I don't believe so."

"Ever hear of him?" Mason asked.

She shook her head, leading the way up a flight of steps. "No," she said over her shoulder, "I'm quite certain I haven't heard of any Jackson Eagan. Why?"

"Jackson Eagan," Mason said, "is the corpse. He registered at the Sleepy Hollow Motel. He was murdered."

"How?"

"A bullet in the head."

"Are they certain?"

"The bullet was still there when the body was exhumed."

"Oh," she said shortly.

She fairly flew up the wide oaken staircase, then hurried down a wide corridor and flung open the door of a spacious corner bedroom. "This is Ted's room," she said.

Mason regarded the framed pictures on the wall—some of them Army pictures, some of them college pictures, a couple of gaudy pin-ups. There were pictures of girls fastened to the sides of the big mirror.

In one corner of the room was a gun cabinet with glass doors. Another locker contained an assortment of golf clubs and two tennis rackets in presses.

Mason tried the door of the gun cabinet. It was locked.

"Got a key to this?" he asked her.

She shook her head. "I don't know much about this room, Mr. Mason. If it's locked, Ted would have the only key."

Mason studied the lock for a moment, then opened his penknife and started pushing with the point against the latch of a spring lock, biting the point of the knife into the brass, and moving the lock back as far as he could.

"I've got to have something to hold this lock," he said after a moment.

"How about a nail file?" Della Street asked, producing a nail file from her purse.

"That should do it," Mason said.

He continued prying the latch back with his knife, holding it in position with the point of the nail file until he could get another purchase on the lock with the knife point. After a few moments the latch clicked back and the door swung open.

Mason hurriedly inspected the small-caliber rifles, paying no attention to the shotguns or the high-powered rifles.

"Well?" she asked, as Mason smelled the barrels.

"None of them seems to have been freshly fired," Mason said. "Of course, they could have been cleaned."

He opened a drawer in the cabinet, disclosing half a dozen revolvers. He pounced on a .22 automatic, smelled the end of the barrel thoughtfully.

"Well?" Mrs. Balfour asked.

Mason said, "This could be it."

He replaced the .22, pushed the drawer shut, closed the glass doors of the cabinet. The spring lock latched into place.

Mason opened the door to the tile bathroom, looked inside, opened the door of the medicine cabinet, opened the door of the closet, and regarded the long array of suits.

"There had been a going-away party in honor of your husband and you the night of September nineteenth?" Mason asked.

She nodded.

"That's when Ted Balfour got—"

"Became indisposed," she interrupted firmly.

"Became indisposed," Mason said. "Do you know what clothes he was wearing that night?"

She shook her head. "I can't remember."

"Was it informal or black tie?"

"No, it was informal. You see, my husband was leaving on a train for Mexico."

"You accompanied him?"

"Yes. He had intended to go alone and have me ride with

him only as far as the Pasadena-Alhambra station. But at the last minute he changed his mind and asked me to go all the way. I didn't have a thing to wear. I . . . well, I was a little put out.''

Della Street said, ''Good heavens! I can imagine you would be annoyed, starting out without . . . You mean, you didn't have a *thing*?''

''Not even a toothbrush,'' she said. ''I had a compact in my handbag and fortunately I had a very small tube of cream that I use to keep my skin soft when the weather is hot and dry. Aside from that, I just had the clothes I was standing in. Of course, it wasn't too bad. I was able to pick up an outfit at El Paso, and then I got some more clothes at Chihuahua.

''My husband is an ardent enthusiast when it comes to his particular hobby. He had received some information on new discoveries to be made in the Tarahumare country in Mexico. Those Tarahumare Indians are very primitive and they live in a wild country, a region of so-called barrancas, which are like our Grand Canyon, only there are hundreds and hundreds of miles of canyon—''

''What's this?'' Mason asked, pouncing on a heavy, square package at the far end of the closet.

''Heavens! I don't know. It looks like some kind of an instrument.''

''It's a tape recorder,'' Mason said, ''and here's something else that apparently goes with it. Does Ted go in for hi-fi?''

She shook her head. ''Not unless it's something new with him. He's not much on music. He goes in more and more for outdoor sports. He wanted to go with my husband on this trip, and Guthrie almost decided to take him, but because of Addison's condition and because my husband felt that Addison wouldn't like having Ted go on the expedition, it was decided Ted should remain here. I now wish to heaven we'd taken him!''

''Ted didn't like the decision?''

''He was very disappointed, Mr. Mason.''

"All right," Mason said. "Let's be brutally frank. Do you have an alibi for the night of the nineteenth?"

"Heavens, yes, the best in the world. I was on the train with my husband."

"Well," Mason said, "you may be asked—"

He broke off as chimes sounded through the house.

Mason said, "That may be the police. Are there back stairs?"

She nodded.

Mason said, "We'll go down the back way. Della, you get my car, drive it around to the garage. I'll get in the car in the garage. Don't tell the officers anything about the stuff I've taken, Mrs. Balfour. You'd better go and talk with them yourself."

Mrs. Balfour flashed him a smile. "We have the utmost confidence in you, Mr. Mason. The whole family does." She glided out of the room.

"Still using her hips," Della Street said.

"Never mind that," Mason told her. "Grab that other package. I'll take this."

"Chief, are we supposed to do this?"

"It depends on how you look at it," Mason told her. "Come on. Let's get down the back stairs. I'll walk over to the garage. Della, you walk around the front of the house very innocently and very leisurely. If there's an officer sitting in the car out in front, flash him a smile. If the car is empty, as I hope will be the case, you can be in a little more of a hurry than you would otherwise. Drive back to the garage, pick me up and we'll get out of here."

Mason carried the heavy tape recorder down the back stairs. Della Street carried the smaller package.

They made an exit through the kitchen, down the steps of the service porch. Mason hurried out toward the garage. Della Street swung to the left around the house, her feet crunching gravel as she walked with a quick, brisk step.

"More casually," Mason cautioned.

She nodded and slowed down.

Mason turned toward the garage, entered and waited until he saw the car, with Della Street at the wheel, come sweeping around the driveway.

"Police?" Mason asked.

She nodded. "It's a police car. Red spotlight. Intercommunicating system and—"

"Anyone in it?"

"No."

Mason grinned. "That's a break."

He opened the rear door of the car, put the tape recorder and the other square package on the back floor, slammed the door shut, jumped in beside Della and said, "Let's go!"

Della Street swung the car in a swift circle, poured gas into the motor as she swept down the curving driveway.

"Okay," Mason cautioned. "Take it easier now as we come out on this road. Don't try to make a left turn. We may run into more police cars. Turn right and then make another right turn a mile or so down here. That'll be Chestnut Street and that will bring us to Sycamore Road. We can get back on that."

Della made a right turn as she left the driveway.

Perry Mason, looking back through the rear window of the car, suddenly whirled his head, settled down in the seat.

"Something?" Della Street asked.

"Two police cars just turning in from the State Highway," Mason said. "Apparently we made it in the nick of time."

Chapter 11

Back in his office Mason found a jubilant Paul Drake.

"We're ahead of the police all the way, Perry."

"How come?"

"That car Jackson Eagan rented," Drake said, "there was a driver's license number on the records."

"What was it?"

"License number Z490553," Drake said.

"Able to trace it?"

"There again we had success. I got in touch with my correspondent in Sacramento. He rushed a man down to the motor vehicle department. That is the number of a driver's license issued to Jackson Eagan, who lives in Chico, a city about two hundred miles north of San Francisco in the Sacramento Valley."

"You have the address?"

"I have the address," Drake said. "I have the guy's physical description from the driver's license and our correspondent in Chico is checking on Jackson Eagan right now."

"What's the description?" Mason asked.

Drake read off his notes: "Male, age 35, height 5 feet 10 inches, weight 175 pounds, hair dark, eyes blue."

"That helps," Mason said. "Now tell me, Paul, what the devil is this?"

Mason removed the cover from the tape recorder.

"That's a darn good grade of a high-fidelity tape recorder," Drake said. "It has variable speeds. It will work at one and seven-eighths inches a second, or at three and three-quarter inches a second. At one and seven-eighths inches a second it will run for three hours on one side of a spool of long-playing tape.''

"You understand how this particular model works?'' Mason asked.

"Perfectly. We use them in our work right along. This is a high-grade model.''

"All right,'' Mason said, "let's see what's recorded on this tape.''

"It's the latest long-playing tape,'' Drake said, plugging in the machine. "You get an hour on one of these spools at three and three-quarter inches to the second, or an hour and a half if you use the long-playing tape. At one and seven-eighths inches per second you get three hours on one side of the tape.''

"What's the reason for the difference in speed?'' Mason asked.

"Simply a question of fidelity. You use seven and a half inches for music, three and three-quarter inches for the human voice where you want high fidelity, but you can get a very satisfactory recording at one and seven-eighths.''

"Okay,'' Mason said. "Let's see what's on the tape.''

"I guess the machine's warmed up enough now,'' Drake said.

He threw a switch.

The spool of tape began to revolve slowly, the tape being taken up on the other spool, feeding through the listening head on the machine.

"Seems to be nothing,'' Drake said after a moment.

"Keep on,'' Mason said. "Let's be certain.''

They sat watching the tape slowly move through the head of the machine for some three or four minutes.

Drake shook his head. "Nothing on it, Perry.''

Mason regarded the machine in frowning contemplation.

"Of course,'' Drake said, "there might be something on the other side. This is a half-track recording. You record on one side of the tape, then reverse the spools and record on the other half of the tape. That is, the recording track is divided into two segments and—"

"Reverse it," Mason said. "Let's see if there's something on the other track."

Drake stopped the machine, reversed the spool. Again the tape fed through the head of the machine, again there was nothing until suddenly a woman's voice coming from the machine said, ". . . fed up with the whole thing myself. You can stand only so much of this gilded—" There followed complete silence.

Drake manipulated the controls on the machine. There was no further sound.

"Well?" Mason asked.

Drake shook his head. "I don't get it."

"Let's take a look at this other box," Mason said. "What's that?"

Drake opened the box. His eyes suddenly glistened with appreciation. "This," he said. "is *really* something."

"All right, what is it?"

"A wall snooper," Drake said.

"What's that, Paul?"

"A very sensitive mike with an electric boosting device. You fasten it to a wall and sounds of conversation in the next room that you can't even hear come in on this mike, are amplified and go on the tape. Then you can plug in earphones, and as the tape goes through a second head, you can hear what's been recorded.

"That's the reason for what we heard on the tape, Perry. The device had been used for a snooping job, then the tape had been fed through the erasing head. They quit erasing on the last few inches of the second half-track and a few words were left."

Mason thought that over. "Why would Ted Balfour have been doing a snooping job, Paul?"

"Perhaps a gag," Drake said. "Perhaps a girlfriend. It could be any one of a hundred things, Perry."

80

Mason nodded. "It could even be that he was checking up on his uncle's new model wife," he said.

"And the job wound up in murder?" Drake asked.

"Or the job wound up by his having a murder wished on him," Mason observed.

Knuckles tapped on the exit door of Mason's private office.

"That's my secretary," Drake said, listening to the rhythm of the code knock.

Della Street opened the door.

"Please give this to Mr. Drake," the secretary said, handing Della a sheet of paper on which there was a typewritten message.

Della Street handed it across to Paul Drake.

"Well, I'll be damned," Drake said.

"What is it?" Mason asked.

"Telegram from my correspondent in Chico. Listen to this:

"JACKSON EAGAN WELL-KNOWN TRAVEL WRITER RESIDING THIS CITY. MOVED AWAY. HAD TROUBLE TRACING, BUT FINALLY FOUND RESIDED BRIEFLY AT MERCED THEN WENT TO YUCATÁN, WHERE HE DIED TWO YEARS AGO. BODY SHIPPED HOME FOR BURIAL. CLOSED COFFIN. WIRE INSTRUCTIONS."

Drake ran his fingers through his hair. "Well, Perry, now we've had everything. Here's a case where the corpse died twice."

Mason nodded to Della Street. "Get out blanks for a petition for habeas corpus," he said. "We're going to file a habeas corpus for Ted Balfour. I have a hunch that it's up to me to work out a legal gambit which will keep the real facts in this case from ever being brought out."

"How the hell are you going to do that?" Drake asked.

Mason grinned. "There's a chance, Paul."

"One chance in a million," Drake said.

"Make it one in five," Mason told him. "And let's hope it works, Paul, because I have a feeling that the true facts in this case are so loaded with explosive they could touch off a chain reaction."

Chapter 12

Judge Cadwell assumed his seat on the bench, glanced down at the courtroom and said, "Now, this is on habeas corpus in the case of Theodore Balfour. A petition was filed, a writ of habeas corpus issued, and this is the hearing on the habeas corpus. I assume that the writ was applied for in connection with the usual practice by which an attorney who is denied the right to communicate with a client applies for a writ of habeas corpus to force the hand of the prosecutor."

Roger Farris, the deputy district attorney, arose and said, "That is correct, Your Honor. We have now filed a complaint on the defendant, accusing him of the crime of murder of one Jackson Eagan, who was then and there a human being, the murder committed with premeditation and malice afore-thought, making the crime first-degree murder.

"The prosecution has no objection to Mr. Perry Mason, as attorney for the defendant, interviewing the defendant at all seasonable and reasonable times."

"I take it then," Judge Cadwell said, glancing down at Perry Mason, "it may be stipulated that the writ can be vacated and the defendant remanded to the custody of the sheriff."

"No, Your Honor," Mason said.

"What?" Judge Cadwell rasped.

"No such stipulation," Mason said.

"Well, the Court will make that ruling anyway," Judge Cadwell snapped. "It would certainly seem that if this man is charged with murder— Now, wait a minute. The Court will not accept the statement of the prosecutor to that effect.

You had better be sworn as a witness, Mr. Prosecutor, unless the facts appear in the return to the writ on file in this court.''

''They do, Your Honor. The facts are undisputed. Even if they weren't, the Court could take judicial cognizance of its own records.''

''Very well,'' Judge Cadwell said.

''May I be heard?'' Mason asked.

''I don't see what you have to be heard about, Mr. Mason. You surely don't contend that where a petitioner has been formally charged with the crime of first-degree murder and has been duly booked on that crime that he is entitled to be released on habeas corpus, do you?''

''In this case, Your Honor, yes.''

''What's the idea?'' Judge Cadwell asked. ''Are you being facetious with the Court, Mr. Mason?''

''No, Your Honor.''

''Well, state your position.''

''The Constitution,'' Mason said, ''provides that no man shall be twice put in jeopardy for the same offense. Your Honor quite recently reviewed the evidence in the case of People versus Balfour and found him guilty of involuntary manslaughter.''

''That was committed with an automobile,'' Judge Cadwell said. ''As I understand it, this is an entirely different case.''

''It may be an entirely different case,'' Mason said, ''but the prosecution is barred because this man has already been tried and convicted of the crime of killing this same Jackson Eagan.''

''Now just a minute,'' Judge Cadwell said as the prosecutor jumped to his feet. ''Let me handle this, Mr. Prosecutor.

''Mr. Mason, do you contend that because the People mistakenly assumed that this was a hit-and-run case and prosecuted the defendant under such a charge, the People are now barred from prosecuting him for first-degree murder—a murder which, so far as the record in the present case

84

discloses, was perpetrated with a lethal weapon? I take it that is a correct statement, is it not, Mr. Prosecutor?''

"It is, Your Honor," Roger Farris said. "It is our contention that Jackson Eagan was killed with a bullet which penetrated his brain and caused almost instant death. We may state that the evidence supporting our position is completely overwhelming. The bullet went into the head but did not emerge from the head. The bullet was found in the brain when the body was exhumed and that bullet has been compared by ballistics experts with a weapon found in the bedroom of Theodore Balfour, the defendant herein, a weapon which was the property of the defendant. The fatal bullet was discharged from that weapon.

"It was quite apparent what happened. An attempt was made to dispose of the victim by having it appear that the man had died as the result of a hit-and-run accident.

"We are perfectly willing, if Mr. Mason wishes, to move to dismiss the former charge of involuntary manslaughter against Mr. Balfour so that he can be prosecuted on a charge of first-degree murder.''

"I don't request any such thing," Mason said. "The defendant has been tried, convicted, and sentenced for the death of Jackson Eagan.''

"Now just a minute," Judge Cadwell said. "The Court is very much concerned with this point raised by Mr. Mason. The Court feels that point is without merit. A man who has been tried for involuntary manslaughter committed with a car cannot claim that such prosecution is a bar to prosecution for first-degree murder committed with a gun.''

"Why not?" Mason asked.

"Why not!" Judge Cadwell shouted. "Because it's absurd. It's ridiculous on the face of it.''

"Would the Court like to hear authorities?" Mason asked.

"The Court would very much like to hear authorities," Judge Cadwell said, "if you have any that bear upon any such case as this.''

"Very well," Mason said. "The general rule is that where

a person is indicted for murder, the charge includes manslaughter. In other words, if a man is charged with first-degree murder it is perfectly permissible for a jury to find him guilty of manslaughter.''

"That is elemental," Judge Cadwell said. "You certainly don't need to cite authorities on any such elemental law point, Mr. Mason."

"I don't intend to," Mason said. "It therefore follows that if a man is tried for first-degree murder and is acquitted, he cannot subsequently be prosecuted for manslaughter involving the same victim."

"That also is elemental," Judge Cadwell said. "The Court doesn't want to waste its time or the time of counsel listening to any authorities on such elemental points."

"Then perhaps," Mason said, "Your Honor would be interested in the Case of People versus McDaniels, 137 Cal. 192 69 Pacific 1006 92 American State Reports 81 59 L.R.A. 578, in which it was held that while an acquittal for a higher offense is a bar to any prosecution for a lower offense necessarily contained in the charge, the converse is also true, and that conviction for a lower offense necessarily included in the higher is a bar to subsequent prosecution for the higher.

"The Court should also study the Case of People versus Krupa, 64 C.A. 2nd 592 149 Pacific 2nd 416, and the Case of People versus Tenner, 67 California Appellate 2nd 360 154 Pacific 2nd page 9, wherein it was held that while Penal Code Section 1023 in terms applies where the prosecution for the higher offense is first, the same rule applies where the prosecution for the lesser offense comes first.

"It was also held in the Case of People versus Ny Sam Chung, 94 Cal. 304 29 Pacific 642 28 American State Reports 129, that a prosecution for a minor offense is a bar to the same act subsequently charged as a higher crime."

Judge Cadwell regarded Mason with frowning contemplation for a moment, then turned to the prosecutor. "Are the people prepared on this point?" he asked.

Roger Farris shook his head. "Your Honor," he said, "I

am not prepared upon this point because, frankly, it never occurred to me. If it had occurred to me, I would have instantly dismissed it from my mind as being too utterly absurd to warrant any serious consideration."

Judge Cadwell nodded. "The Court feels that the point must be without merit," he said. "Even if it has some merit, the Court would much rather commit error in deciding the case according to justice and the equities, rather than permit what might be a deliberate murder to be condoned because of a pure technicality."

"I would like to suggest to the Court," Mason said, "that it would be interesting to know the theory of the prosecution. Is it the theory of the prosecution that if the jury in this case should return a verdict of guilty of manslaughter, and the Court should sentence the defendant to prison, the prosecution could then file another charge of murder against the defendant and secure a second punishment?"

"Certainly not!" Farris snapped.

"If you had prosecuted this man for murder originally," Mason said, "and the jury had returned a verdict of not guilty, would it be your position that you could again prosecute him on a charge of involuntary manslaughter?"

"That would depend," Farris said, suddenly becoming cautious. "It would depend on the facts."

"Exactly," Mason said, grinning. "Once a defendant has been placed on trial, jeopardy has attached. Once the defendant has been convicted and sentenced, he has paid the penalty demanded by law. If the prosecution, as a result of poor judgment, poor investigative work, or poor thinking, charges the man with a lesser offense than it subsequently thinks it might be able to prove, the prior case is nevertheless a bar to a prosecution for a higher offense at a later date."

Judge Cadwell said, "The Court is going to take a sixty-minute recess. The Court wants to look up some of these authorities. This is a most unusual situation, a most astounding situation. I may state that as soon as I heard the contention of the defendant, I felt that the absurdity of that contention was so great that it amounted to sheer legal frivolity. But now that I think the matter over and appreciate the force of the defendant's contention, it appears that there may well be merit to it.

"Looking at it from a broad standpoint, the defendant was charged with unlawful acts causing the death of Jackson Eagan. To be certain, those acts were of an entirely different nature from the acts now complained of, but they brought about the same result, to wit, the unlawful death of Jackson Eagan.

"The defendant was prosecuted on that charge and he was convicted. Is it possible, Mr. Prosecutor, that this whole situation was an elaborate setup by the defendant in order to escape the penalties of premeditated murder?"

"I don't know, Your Honor," Farris said. "I certainly wouldn't want to make a definite charge, but here is a situation where legal ingenuity of a high order seems to have been used to trap the prosecution into a most unusual situation. Looking back on the evidence in that hit-and-run case, it would seem almost a suspicious circumstance that the witness, Myrtle Anne Haley, so promptly and obligingly wrote down the license number of the car of the defendant, Ted Balfour.

"The situation is all the more significant when one remembers that the witness in question is employed by a subsidiary of the Balfour Allied Associates. Frankly, our office was amazed when she came forward as such a willing informant."

Judge Cadwell pursed his lips, looked down at Perry Mason thoughtfully. "There *is* some evidence here of legal ingenuity of a high order," he said. "However, present counsel did not try that hit-and-run case."

"But present council did sit in court after the case got under way," Farris pointed out. "He did not sit in the bar, but sat as a spectator—a very interested spectator."

Judge Cadwell looked once more at Perry Mason.

"I object to these innuendoes, Your Honor," Mason said.

"If the prosecution can prove any such preconceived plan or conspiracy on the part of the defendant to mislead the authorities and bring about a trial for a lesser charge, the situation will be different; but it would have to amount to a fraud on the Court brought about with the connivance of the defendant, and there would have to be *proof* to establish that point."

"The Court will take a sixty-minute recess," Judge Cadwell said. "The Court wants to look into these things. This is a most unusual situation, a very unusual situation. The Court is very reluctant to think that any interpretation of the law could be such that a defense of one in jeopardy could, under circumstances such as these, prevent a prosecution for first-degree murder."

"And may the Court make an order that I be permitted to communicate with the defendant during the recess?" Mason asked. "The defendant was arrested and has been held incommunicado so far as any worthwhile communication with counsel, with family or friends is concerned."

"Very well," Judge Cadwell ruled. "The sheriff will take such precautions as he may see fit, but during the recess of the Court Mr. Mason will be permitted to communicate with his client as much as he may desire."

"I can put the defendant in the witness room," the deputy said, "and Mr. Mason can communicate with him there."

"Very well," Judge Cadwell said. "I don't care how you do it, but it must be a communication under such circumstances that the defendant can disclose any defense he may have to the charge and have an opportunity to receive confidential advice from his attorney. That means that no attempt should be made to audit the conversation in any manner.

"Court will take a recess for one hour."

Mason motioned to Ted Balfour. "Step this way, if you please, Mr. Balfour."

Roger Farris, his face showing his consternation, hurried to the law library in a panic of apprehension.

Chapter 13

Balfour, a tall, wavy-haired young man who seemed ill at ease, seated himself across the table from Perry Mason. "Is there any chance you can get me out of this mess without my having to go on the witness stand?"

Mason nodded.

"That would be wonderful, Mr. Mason."

Mason studied the young man. He saw a big-boned, flat-waisted individual whose slow-speaking, almost lethargic manner seemed somehow to serve as a most effective mask behind which the real personality was concealed from the public gaze.

Mason said, "Suppose you tell me the truth about what happened on the night of September nineteenth and the early morning of September twentieth."

Balfour passed a hand over his forehead. "Lord, how I wish I knew!" he said.

"Start talking and tell me everything you do know," Mason said impatiently. "You're not dealing with the police now. I'm your lawyer and I have to know what we're up against."

Ted Balfour shifted his position. He cleared his throat, ran an awkward hand through his thick, wavy, dark hair.

"Go on," Mason snapped. "Quit stalling for time. Start talking!"

"Well," Ted Balfour said, "Uncle Guthrie was going to Mexico. He was going into the Tarahumare country. He's been down there before, sort of scratching the surface, as he expressed it. This time he wanted to get down in some of the barrancas that were so inaccessible that it was reasonable to suppose no other white man had ever been in there."

"Such country exists?"

"Down in that part of Mexico it does."

"All right. What happened?"

"Well, Dorla was going to ride as far as Pasadena with him, just to make sure that he got on the train and had his tickets and everything and that there were no last-minute instructions. She was to get off at the Alhambra-Pasadena station, but at the last minute Uncle Guthrie decided he wanted her with him and told her she'd better go along."

"How long has she been married to your uncle?"

"A little over two years."

"How long have you been home from the Army?"

"A little over four months."

"You have seen a good deal of her?"

"Well, naturally, we're all living in the same house."

"She's friendly?"

"Yes."

"At any time has she seemed to be overly friendly?"

"What do you mean by that?" Balfour asked, straightening up with a certain show of indignation.

"Figure it out," Mason told him. "It's a simple question, and any show of righteous indignation on your part will be a damn good indication to me that there's something wrong."

Ted Balfour seemed to wilt in the chair.

"Go on," Mason said, "answer the question. Was there any indication of overfriendliness?"

Balfour took a deep breath. "I don't know."

"What the hell do you mean, you don't know?" Mason blazed. "Come clean!"

"Uncle Guthrie and Uncle Addison wouldn't like your questions or your manner, if you don't mind my saying so, Mr. Mason."

"To hell with your uncles!" Mason said. "I'm trying to keep *you* from going to the gas chamber for first-degree murder. As your attorney, I have to know the facts. I want to know what I'm up against."

"The gas chamber!" Ted Balfour exclaimed.

"Sure. What did you think they did with murderers? Did you think they slapped their wrists or cut off their allowances for a month?"

"But I . . . I didn't do a thing. I don't know anything about this man, Jackson Eagan. I never met him. I surely didn't kill him or anyone else."

Mason's eyes bored into those of the young man. "Did Dorla become too friendly?"

Ted Balfour sighed. "Honest, Mr. Mason, I can't answer that question."

"What do you mean, you can't answer it?"

"Frankly, I don't know."

"Why don't you know?"

"Well, at times I'd think . . . well . . . it's hard to explain what I mean. She sometimes seems to sort of presume on the relationship, and I'd think she . . . and then again, it would be . . . It's something I just don't know."

"What did she do?"

"Well, she'd run in and out."

"Of your room?"

"Yes. It would be different if she were really my aunt. But she's not related at all, and . . . well, there's not any way of really describing what I mean."

"You never tried to find out? You never made a pass?"

"Heavens, no! I always treated her just as an aunt, but she'd run in and out, and occasionally I'd see her— One night when Uncle Guthrie was away and she thought she heard a noise downstairs, she came to my room to ask me if I'd heard it. It was bright moonlight and she had on a thin, filmy night-gown . . . and she said she was frightened."

"What did you do?"

"I told her she was nervous and to go back to bed and lock her bedroom door. I said even if someone were downstairs he couldn't bother her if she kept her door bolted, and all the stuff was insured."

"Did your uncle ever get jealous?"

"Of me?"

"Yes."

"Heavens, no!"

"Is he happy?"

"I've never asked him. He's never confided in me. He's pretty much occupied with his hobby."

"Look here," Mason said. "Was your uncle *ever* jealous of anyone?"

"Not that I know. He kept his feelings pretty much to himself."

"Did he ever ask you to check on Dorla in any way?"

"Gosh, no! He wouldn't have done that."

"Suppose he had been jealous. Suppose he thought she was two-timing him?"

"That would be different."

"All right," Mason said. "You have a tape recording machine with a special microphone that's built to flatten up against a wall. Why did you have that and who told you to get it?"

Ted Balfour looked at him blankly.

"Go on," Mason said. "Where did you get it?"

"I never got it, Mr. Mason. I don't have it."

"Don't be silly," Mason told him. "You have it. It was in your closet. I took it out. Now tell me, how did it get there?"

"Somebody must have put it there. It wasn't mine."

"You know I'm your lawyer?"

"Yes."

"And I'm trying to help you?"

"Yes."

"No matter what you've done, you tell me what it is and I'll do my best to help you. I'll see that you get the best deal you can get, no matter what it is. You understand that?"

"Yes, sir."

"But you mustn't lie to me."

"Yes, sir."

"All right. Have you been lying?"

"No, sir."

"You've told me the truth?"

"Yes, sir."

Mason said, "Let's go back to the night of the nineteenth. Now what happened?"

My uncle was leaving for Mexico. Dorla was going with him as far as Pasadena. Then Uncle Guthrie changed his mind at the last minute and took Dorla with him. He's funny that way. He has a restless mind. He'll be all enthused about something or some idea, and then he'll change. He'll have a car and like it first rate and then something will happen and he'll trade it in on a new model, usually of a different make."

"Would he feel that way about women?"

"I guess so, but Aunt Martha died, so he didn't have to trade anything in. I mean, Dorla was a new model. She appealed to him as soon as he saw her."

"I'll bet she did," Mason said.

Ted Balfour seemed apologetic. "I guess that after Aunt Martha died the family sort of expected Uncle Guthrie would marry Florence Ingle. She's a mighty fine woman and they've been friends. But Dorla came along and . . . well, that's the way it was."

"You don't call her 'Aunt Dorla'?"

"No."

"Why?"

"She doesn't want me to. She says it makes her seem . . . she used a funny word."

"What was it?"

"De-sexified."

"So at the last minute and because of something that may have happened on the train, your uncle decided he wouldn't let her stay behind in the same house with you?"

"Oh, it wasn't that! He just decided to take her with him."

"And she didn't have any clothes with her?"

94

"No, sir. She purchased things in El Paso."

"Did you go to the station to see your uncle and Dorla off?"

"Yes, sir."

"Who else went?"

"Three or four of his intimate friends."

"How about Marilyn Keith, Addison Balfour's secretary, was she there?"

"She showed up at the last minute with a message Uncle Addison asked her to deliver. She wasn't there to see him off exactly, but to give him the message."

"Then what happened?"

"Well, there'd been something of a going-away party before."

"Where was this party held?"

"At Florence Ingle's place."

"Is she interested in archaeology?"

"I guess so. She's interested in things my uncle is interested in."

"She knew your uncle for some time before he married Dorla?"

"Oh, yes."

"And your uncle's close friends felt he might marry this Florence Ingle?"

"That's what I've heard."

"How does Florence like Dorla?"

"All right, I guess. She's always very sweet to her."

"Ted, look at me. Look me in the eyes. Now tell me, how does she like Dorla?"

Ted took a deep breath. "She hates Dorla's guts."

"That's better. Now, Florence Ingle gave this party?"

"Yes."

"And you put your uncle and Dorla aboard the train; that is, some of you did?"

"Yes."

"You left the party to do that?"

"Yes."

"Where did they take the train?"

"At the Arcade station."

"And then you went back to the party?"

"Yes."

"Dorla was to get off the train at the Alhambra-Pasadena station?"

"Yes, sir."

"And how was she to get back?"

"By taxicab. She was to go back to the house . . . you know, her house."

"You went back to the Florence Ingle party?"

"Yes."

"Now, did Marilyn Keith go back there?"

"Yes, she did. Mrs. Ingle invited her to come along, and she did."

"Did you talk with her?"

"Mrs. Ingle?"

"No, Marilyn Keith."

"Some . . . not much. She's a very sweet girl and very intelligent."

"All this was after dinner?"

"Yes, sir."

"About what time was it when you got back there?"

"I'd say about . . . oh, I don't know. I guess it was around eight-thirty or nine o'clock when we got back to Florence Ingle's house."

"And how late did you stay?"

"I remember there was some dancing and a little talk and the party began to break up pretty early."

"How many people were there?"

"Not too many. Around eighteen or twenty, I guess."

"And you were not driving your sports car?"

"No, I was driving the big car."

"Why?"

"Because I was taking Uncle to the train and his baggage was in the car."

96

"All right. What happened after you went back to the party?"

"I had two or three drinks, not many. But along about ten o'clock I had a Scotch and soda, and I think that almost immediately after I drank that I knew something was wrong with me."

"In what way?"

"I began to see double and . . . well, I was sick."

"What did you do?"

"I wanted to get out in the open air. I went out and sat in the car for a while and then I don't know . . . the next thing I knew I came to in the car. I haven't told anyone else, but Marilyn Keith was driving."

"Did you talk with her?"

"I asked her what had happened, and she told me to keep quiet and I'd be all right."

"Then what?"

"I remember being terribly weak. I put my head over on her shoulder and passed out."

"Then what?"

"The next thing I knew I was in bed. It was four thirty-five."

"You looked at your watch?"

"Yes."

"Were you undressed?"

"Yes."

"In pajamas?"

"Yes."

"Do you remember undressing?"

"No."

"Did you go out again after Marilyn Keith took you home?"

"Mr. Mason, I wish I knew. I haven't told anybody else this, but I just don't know. I must have."

"Why do you say you must have?"

"Because I had the key to the car."

"What do you mean?"

"It was in my trousers pocket."

"Isn't that where you usually keep it?"

"That's where *I* usually keep the key to my car. Whenever I run the car in, I take the key out and put it in my trousers pocket; but I don't think Marilyn Keith would have put it there."

"You don't leave the cars with keys in them in the garage?"

"No. Everyone in the family has his own key to each of the cars."

"How well do you know Marilyn Keith?"

"I've seen her a few times in my uncle's office. That's all."

"Ever been out with her?"

"No."

"Do you like her?"

"I do now. I'd never noticed her very much before. She's Uncle Addison's secretary. She'd always smile at me and tell me to go right in whenever I went up to visit Uncle Addison. I never noticed her as a woman or thought about her in that way. Then at the party I got talking with her socially and I realized she was really beautiful. Later on, when I got sick . . . I can't describe it, Mr. Mason. Something happened. I was leaning on her—I must have been an awful nuisance— and she was so sweet about it, so competent, so considerate. She was sweet."

"She put you to bed?"

"She took me up to my room."

"You suddenly realized you liked her?"

"Yes."

"A little more about Florence Ingle—was she married when your uncle first knew her?"

"Yes."

"What happened to her husband?"

"He was killed."

"Where?"

"In a plane crash."

"A transport plane?"

"No, a private plane. He was doing some kind of prospecting."

"So Mrs. Ingle became a widow, and how long was that before your aunt died?"

"Oh, six months or so, I guess."

"And after that Florence Ingle resumed her friendship with your uncle?"

"Yes."

"Then Dorla came along and whisked your uncle right out from under Mrs. Ingle's nose?"

"I guess so. I wouldn't want to say."

"Is there anything else that you think I should know?"

"Just one thing."

"What?"

"The speedometer on the big car."

"What about it?"

"There was too much mileage on it."

"When?"

"The next morning."

"Why did you notice that?"

"Because I noticed the mileage when we were at the station. The car had to be serviced and I was going to get it serviced. It had turned up an even ten thousand miles as I was driving to the station, and my uncle remarked about it and said that I was to get it serviced. There shouldn't have been over another twenty or twenty-five miles on it at the most."

"But there was more on it?"

"I'll say there was."

"How much more?"

"As nearly as I could work it out, about twenty-five miles too much."

"Did you tell anyone about this?"

"No, sir."

"Did you tell Howland about it?"

"No, sir."

"Tell Howland about any of this stuff we've been discussing?"

"No, sir. Howland told me that he didn't want me to tell him anything until he asked me. He said that he liked to fight his cases by picking flaws in the prosecution's case, that if it came to a showdown, where he had to put me on the witness stand, he'd ask me some questions, but he didn't want to know the answers until that became necessary."

"So you didn't tell him anything?"

"No, sir. I told him I hadn't hit anyone with the car, and that's all."

"But because you had the key in the pocket of your clothes, and because there was that extra mileage on the car, you think it was taken out again?"

"Yes, sir, because the key was in my *trousers* pocket."

"But how do you know Marilyn Keith drove you straight home? How do you know that she didn't go out somewhere with you in the car and try to wait until you got sobered up somewhat before she took you home, then decided it was no use and drove you back?"

"I don't know, of course."

"All right," Mason said. "You've given me the information I want. Now sit tight."

"What's going to happen, Mr. Mason? Is the judge going to turn me loose?"

"I don't think so."

"Mr. Mason, do you think I . . . do you think I *could* have killed that man? Could have killed anyone?"

"I don't know," Mason said. "Someone got a gun out of your cabinet, killed a man, put in fresh shells, and replaced the gun."

Ted Balfour said, "I can't understand it. I . . . I *hope* I didn't go out again."

"If you had, you certainly wouldn't have taken the gun."

The young man's silence caught Mason's attention.

"Would you?" he snapped.

"I don't know."

"What about that gun?" Mason said. "Did you have it with you?"

"It was in the glove compartment of the car."

"The hell it was!"

Balfour nodded.

"Now you tell me *why* you had that gun in the glove compartment," Mason said.

"I was afraid."

"Of what?"

"I'd been doing some gambling . . . cards. I got in too deep. I was in debt. I'd been threatened. They were going to send a collector. You know what that is, Mr. Mason . . . when the boys send a collector. The first time he just beats you up. After that . . . well, you have to pay."

Mason regarded the young man with eyes that showed sheer exasperation. "Why the hell didn't you tell me about this before?"

"I was ashamed."

"Did you tell the police about having the .22 in the car?"

Balfour shook his head.

"About the gambling?"

"No."

"Did you tell them about the mileage on the speedometer or about having the key to the car in your pocket?"

"No, sir, I didn't."

"When did you take the gun out of the glove compartment and put it back in the gun cabinet?"

"I don't know. I wish I did. That's another reason I feel certain I must have taken the car out again after Marilyn Keith took me home. Next morning, the gun was in the gun case in the drawer where it belongs. Marilyn certainly wouldn't have taken the gun out of the glove compartment. Even if she had, she wouldn't know where I keep it. It had been put right back in its regular place in the gun cabinet."

Mason frowned. "You could be in one hell of a fix on this case."

"I know."

"All right," Mason said. "Sit tight. Don't talk with anyone. Don't answer any questions the police may ask you. They probably won't try to get any more information out of you. If they do, refer them to me. Tell them I'm your lawyer and that you're not talking."

"And you don't think the judge will turn me loose on this technicality?"

Mason shook his head. "He's struggling between his concept of the law and his conscience. He won't turn you loose."

"Why did you raise the point?"

"To throw a scare into the prosecutor," Mason said. "They know now they have a monkey wrench in the machinery which may strip a few gears at any time. You're just going to have to stand up and take it from now on, Ted."

"I'll stand up and take it, Mr. Mason, but I sure would like to know what happened. I— Gosh! I can't believe that . . . well, I just *couldn't* have killed the man, that's all."

"Sit tight," Mason said. "Don't talk with newspaper reporters, don't talk with police, don't talk with anyone unless I'm present. I'll be seeing you."

Thirty minutes later Judge Cadwell returned to court and proceeded with the habeas corpus hearing.

"Surprisingly enough, this technical point seems to have some merit," the judge ruled. "It comes as a shock to the Court to think that a defendant could place himself behind such a barricade of legal technicality.

"However, regardless of the letter of the law, there are two points to be considered: I can't dismiss the possibility that this whole situation has been deliberately engineered so there will be a technical defense to a murder charge. The other point is that I feel a higher court should pass on this matter. If I grant the habeas corpus, the defendant will simply go free. If I hold the defendant for trial by denying the writ, the matter can be taken to a higher court on a plea of once in jeopardy.

"Since a plea of once in jeopardy will presumably be made at the time of the trial of the case, it will be among the issues

102

raised at that trial. This court does not intend to pass on the validity of such a plea of once in jeopardy at this time, except insofar as it applies to this writ of habeas corpus. The Court denies the habeas corpus. The prisoner is remanded to the custody of the sheriff.''

Mason's face was expressionless as he left the courtroom. Paul Drake buttonholed him in the corridor.

"You wanted the dope on that tape recorder," Drake said. "I got the serial number, wired the manufacturer, the manufacturer gave me the name of the distributor, the distributor checked his records to the retailer. I finally got what we wanted."

"Okay," Mason said. "Who bought it?"

"A woman by the name of Florence Ingle living out in the Wilshire district. Does that name mean anything to you?"

"It means a lot," Mason said. "Where is Mrs. Ingle now?"

"I thought you'd ask that question," Drake said. "The answer gave us one hell of a job."

"Where is she?"

"She took a plane. Ostensibly she went on to Miami, then to Atlantic City, but the person who went on to Atlantic City wasn't Mrs. Ingle at all. She registered at hotels under the name of Florence Ingle, but it wasn't the same woman."

"Got a description?" Mason asked.

"Florence Ingle is about thirty-eight, well groomed, small-boned, good figure, rich, a good golfer, brunette, large dark eyes, five feet two, a hundred and seventeen pounds, very gracious, runs to diamond jewelry and is lonely in an aristocratic way. She's rather a tragic figure.

"The woman who impersonated Florence Ingle was something like her, but was heavier and didn't know her way around in the high-class places. She was tight-lipped, self-conscious, overdid everything trying to act the part of a wealthy woman. In the course of time she vanished absolutely and utterly, without leaving a trail. She left a lot of

103

baggage in the hotel, but the bill was paid in full, so the hotel is storing the baggage.''

"Never mind all the build-up," Mason asked. "Did your men find out where Florence Ingle is now?"

"Yes. It was a hell of a job, Perry. I want you to understand that—"

"I know, I know," Mason said. "Where is she?"

"Staying at the Mission Inn at Riverside, California, under the name of Florence Landis, which was her maiden name. She's posing as a wealthy widow from the East."

"Now," Mason said, "we're beginning to get somewhere."

Chapter 14

Perry Mason stood at the cigar counter for a few minutes. He lit a cigarette, sauntered across to the outdoor tables by the swimming pool, started toward the entrance of the hotel, thought better of it, stretched, yawned, walked back toward the pool, seated himself in a chair, stretched his long legs out in front of him, and crossed his ankles.

The attractive brunette in the sunsuit who was seated next to him flashed a surreptitious glance from behind her dark glasses at the granite-hard profile. For several seconds she appraised him, then looked away and regarded the swimmers at the pool.

"Would you prefer to talk here or in your room, Mrs. Ingle?" Mason asked in a conversational voice, without even turning to glance at her.

She jumped as though the chair had been wired to give her an electric shock, started to get up, then collapsed back in the chair. "My name," she said, "is Florence Landis."

"That's the name you registered under," Mason said. "It was your maiden name. Your real name is Florence Ingle. You're supposed to be on a vacation in Atlantic City. Do you want to talk here or in your room?"

"I have nothing to talk about."

"I think you have," Mason said. "I'm Perry Mason."

"What do you want to know?"

"I'm representing Ted Balfour. I want to know what you know and I want to know *all* you know."

"I know nothing that would help Ted."

"Then why the run-around?"

"Because, Mr. Mason, what I know would hurt your client. I don't want to do anything to hurt Ted. I'm trying to keep out of the way. Please, *please* don't press me! If you do, you'll be sorry.''

Mason said, ''I'm sorry, but I have to know what you know.''

''I've warned you, Mr. Mason.''

Mason said, ''You can talk to me. You don't have to talk to the prosecution.''

''What makes you think I know anything?''

''When a witness runs away I want to know what she's running from and why.''

''All right,'' she said, ''I'll tell you what it's all about. Ted Balfour killed that man and then tried to make it look like an automobile accident.''

''What makes you think so?''

''Because Ted was in a jam. Ted had an allowance and he couldn't afford to exceed it. He got up against it for money and started playing for high stakes, and then he started plunging. He didn't have the money, but his credit was good and . . . well, it's the old story. His cards didn't come in and Ted was left in a terrific predicament.

''If either one of his uncles had known what he was doing, he would have been disinherited—at least Ted thought so. They had him pretty well scared. Personally, I'm convinced that while they might try to frighten the boy, they never would have gone so far as to disinherit him.''

''Go on,'' Mason said. ''I take it Ted came to you?''

''Ted came to me.''

''What did he tell you?''

''He told me he had to have twenty thousand dollars. He told me that if he didn't get it, it was going to be just too bad.''

''What made him think so?''

''He had a letter that he showed me.''

''A letter from whom?''

''He knew who had written the letter, all right, but it was unsigned.''

106

"Who had written it?"

"The syndicate."

"Go on," Mason said.

"The letter told him that they didn't like welchers. They said that if he didn't get the money, their collector would call."

"Twenty thousand dollars is a lot of money," Mason said.

"He never would have got in that deep if they hadn't played him for a sucker. They let him get in deeper than he could pay and then saw that he was dealt the second-best hands."

"And then when they had him hooked, they lowered the boom? Is that right?"

"That's right."

"Did you come through with the twenty thousand?"

"No, I didn't. I wish I had now. I thought Ted had to be taught a lesson. I felt that if he got the money from me, it wouldn't be any time at all until he'd start trying to get the money to pay me back by betting sure things. I felt it was time for Ted to grow up. Oh, Mr. Mason, if you only knew how I've regretted that decision!

"Ted was sick over the whole thing. He told me he had a .22 automatic in the glove compartment of his car and he intended to use it. He said that he wasn't going to be waylaid and beaten up and then simply tell the police he didn't have any idea who did it. He said that he was good for the money but that it would take him a while to get it together. There was a trust which had been left him by his parents and he thought he could explain the situation to the trustee, but the trustee was on vacation and he had to have a little more time."

"All right," Mason said, "what happened?"

"The dead man must have been the collector," she said. "Don't you see? Ted killed him and then tried to make it look as though the man had been killed in a hit-and-run accident."

Mason studied her thoughtfully for a moment, then said, "You told that readily enough."

"It's the truth."

"I'm sure it is. I merely said, you told it to me readily enough."

"I had to. You've trapped me. I don't know how you found me here, but since you found me, I had to tell you what I know, no matter whom it hurts."

"All right," Mason said. "So far, so good. Now tell me the real reason you went to such pains to keep from being questioned."

"I've told you everything I know."

"What about the tape recorder?"

"What tape recorder?"

"The one you bought—the wall snooper."

"I don't know what you're talking about."

"Come on," Mason said. "Come clean!"

"Mr. Mason, you can't talk to me like that! You must think I'm someone whom you can push around. Your very manner is insulting. I am a truthful woman, and I am not a woman who is accustomed to being pushed around by—"

Mason reached in the inside pocket of his light-weight business suit, pulled out a folded paper, and dropped it in her lap.

"What's that?" she asked.

"Your copy of a subpoena in the case of People versus Balfour. Here's the original, with the signature of the clerk and the seal of the Court. Be there at the time of trial; otherwise be subject to proceedings in contempt of court."

Mason arose, said, "I'm sorry I had to do that, but you brought it on yourself, Mrs. Ingle. Good-by now."

Mason had taken two steps before her voice caught up with him. "Wait, wait, for heaven's sake, Mr. Mason, wait!"

Mason paused, looked back over his shoulder.

"I'll . . . I'll tell you the truth. You can't do this to me, Mr. Mason. You can't! You mustn't!"

"Mustn't do what?"

"Mustn't subpoena me in that case."

"Why?"

108

"Because if you put me on the stand I . . . it will . . . it will be terrible."

"Go ahead," Mason said. "Keep talking."

She stood looking at his stern features, her own face white and frightened. "I don't dare to," she said. "I simply don't dare tell anyone."

"Why not?"

"It's . . . it won't help you, Mr. Mason. It will . . . it will be terrible!"

"All right," Mason said, "you have your subpoena. Be there in court."

"But you can't put me on the stand. If I told about what Ted Balfour had asked me to do, if I told you about his needing the money and the collector—"

"No one would believe you," Mason interrupted. "I've served a subpoena on you. You're trying to get out of circulation. That subpoena is going to smoke you out in the open. The only reason for it is that I want the true story. If you know something that's causing you to take all these precautions, I want to find out what it is."

She looked at him as though she might be about to faint, then, with difficulty composing herself, she said, "Come into the bar where we can talk without my making a spectacle of myself."

"You'll tell me the truth?" Mason asked.

She nodded.

"Let's go," Mason told her, leading the way to the bar.

"Well?" Mason said after the waiter had gone.

"Mr. Mason, I'm protecting someone."

"I was satisfied you were," Mason said.

"Someone whom I love."

"Guthrie Balfour?" Mason asked.

For a moment it appeared she would deny it. Then she tearfully nodded.

"All right," Mason said. "Let's have the truth this time."

"I'm not a good liar, Mr. Mason," she said. "I never had occasion to do much lying."

"I know," Mason said sympathetically.

She had taken off the dark glasses. The eyes that looked at the lawyer were circled with the weariness of sleepless nights and filled with dismay.

"Go on," Mason said. "What happened?"

She said, "Mr. Mason, that Dorla Balfour is a scheming, wicked woman who has almost a hypnotic influence over Guthrie Balfour. She's not his type at all. He's wasting himself on her, and yet somehow . . . well, somehow I wonder if she doesn't have some terrific hold on him, something that he can't escape."

"What makes you think so?" Mason asked.

"She's twisting him around her thumb."

"Go on."

"I'll tell you the real story, Mr. Mason, the whole story. Please listen and don't interrupt. It's a thoroughly incredible story and I'm not proud of my part in it, but . . . well, it will explain a lot of things."

"Go ahead," Mason said.

"Dorla Balfour was and is a little tramp. She was taking Guthrie for everything she could take him for, and, believe me, the minute Guthrie Balfour got out of town, she was putting herself in circulation without missing a minute."

Mason nodded.

"Guthrie had begun to wake up," she said. "He wanted a divorce, but he didn't want to get stuck for a lot of alimony. Dorla wouldn't mind a bit if he'd divorce her, but she has her grasping little hand out for a big slice of alimony. She'd go to the best lawyers in the country and she'd make herself just as much of a legal nuisance as is possible. She'd tie up Guthrie's property. She'd get restraining orders. She'd drag him into court on orders to show cause, and she'd . . . well, she'd raise the devil."

"Meaning that she'd drag your name into it?" Mason asked.

Mrs. Ingle lowered her eyes.

"Yes or no?" Mason asked.

110

"Yes," she said in a low voice. "Only there was nothing . . . nothing except sympathy."

"But you couldn't prove that?" Mason asked.

"She could make nasty insinuations and get notoriety for both of us."

"Okay," Mason said, "now we're doing better. Let's have the story."

"Well, Guthrie was leaving for Chihuahua City; that is, that's what he told her. Actually, he got on the train at Los Angeles and then left it at the Alhambra-Pasadena station."

"*He* left it?" Mason asked.

She nodded.

"Why, that's what Dorla was supposed to have done," Mason said.

"I know," she said. "That was all part of the plan he had worked out. When the train stopped at the Pasadena station, he kissed her good-by and got back aboard the train. The vestibule doors slammed and the train started out. Guthrie sent the porter back on an errand, opened the car door on the other side of the car, and swung to the ground as the train was gathering speed. By the time the train had gone on past, Dorla was in a taxicab."

"And Guthrie?" Mason asked.

"Guthrie jumped in a car he'd rented earlier in the day from a drive-yourself rental agency. He'd parked the car at the station. He followed Dorla."

"Then, when the train pulled out, neither Guthrie nor Dorla was aboard?"

"That's right."

"Go ahead. What happened then?"

"Guthrie followed Dorla. Oh, Mr. Mason, I'd pleaded with him not to do it. I asked him a dozen times to get some private detective agency on the job. That's their business. But Guthrie had to do this himself. I think he was so utterly fascinated by Dorla that he wouldn't believe anything against her unless he saw it with his own eyes.

"I think he knew the truth, but I think he knew himself

111

well enough to feel she'd be able to talk him out of it unless he saw her himself and had the proof. He wanted proof without any outsiders for witnesses. That's why he asked me to get him that tape recorder. He wanted to record what was happening after she . . . well, you know, after she met the man.''

"Go on," Mason said. "What did Dorla do?"

"Drove to the Sleepy Hollow Motel."

"So then what?"

"She met her boyfriend there. They had a passionate reunion."

"Where was Guthrie?"

"He'd managed to get into the unit that adjoined the one where Dorla's boyfriend was staying. He'd put the microphone up to the wall and he had a tape recording of the whole business."

"You were there with him?"

"Good heavens, no! That would have ruined everything he was trying to do."

"That's what I thought, but how do you know all this?"

"He phoned me."

"From Chihuahua?"

"No. Please let me tell it in my own way."

"Go ahead."

"After a while Dorla went out. She said she had to go home and let Ted know she was seeking her virtuous couch. She said that she'd pick up a suitcase and be back later on in the evening."

"Then what?"

"That's where Guthrie made the mistake of his life," she said. "He thought that he might be able to go into the motel unit next door, face this man who was registered under the name of Jackson Eagan and put it up to him cold turkey. He thought that this man might get frightened and sign a statement. It was a crazy thing to do."

"What happened?"

"This man, Eagan, was in a dimly lit motel bedroom. The minute Guthrie walked in Eagan snapped on a powerful

112

flashlight and the beam hit Guthrie right in the face, completely blinding him. Eagan, on the other hand, could see his visitor. He obviously recognized Guthrie, felt certain the irate husband was about to invoke the unwritten law, and threw a chair. He followed it up by hitting the blinded Guthrie with everything he had.

"Guthrie tried to frighten this man by bringing out this gun of Ted's that he'd taken from the glove compartment of the car without Ted's knowing it.

"The two men started fighting for the gun. In the struggle the gun went off and Eagan fell to the floor. Guthrie knew from the way he hit the floor he was dead. And all at once Guthrie realized the full implications of the situation. He was afraid someone might have heard the shot and phoned for the police, so he jumped in his car and drove away fast."

"Then what?"

"Then," she said, "Guthrie had this idea. He realized that nobody, except me, knew that he had left the train. He called me from the telephone in his house. He told me everything that had happened. He said that he was going to take the company plane, fly to Phoenix and pick up the train there. He said he'd wire for Dorla to join him at Tucson, and in that way Dorla would have to give him an alibi. He asked me to take a commercial plane to Phoenix and fly his plane back. He said that he would leave a note with the attendant so that I could get the plane, and if I'd do that, well, no one would ever be the wiser."

"And so?" Mason asked.

"So I did that. I went down to Phoenix the next day. His plane was there and so was the note so that I could get it without any trouble. I flew it back, picked up his rented car where he'd left it at the hangar, and returned it to the rental agency."

"And Dorla joined him?"

"Dorla must have joined him. Only to hear her tell it, she never got off the train. I know that's a lie because I know from Guthrie what really happened. You can see the whole thing, Mr. Mason. He called on her to give him an alibi. He didn't tell her what happened. He didn't need to. When she got her suitcase and returned to the motel, she found her lover boy, Eagan, lying there dead.

"Now, under those circumstances, I know exactly what she'd have done, and it's just what she did. She telephoned for Banner Boles, the ace trouble shooter for Balfour Allied Associates. Boles realized at once that it would be better to have a drunk-driving charge against Ted and try to beat that rap than to have a murder charge against Guthrie. He's unbelievably resourceful and clever.

"So he fixed the whole deal up and Dorla flew to Tucson and picked up the train. Guthrie asked her to swear she'd been on the train all the time. That was right down her alley. Now she has a murder rap on him and she'll bleed him white. There won't be any divorce until she is all ready for it, with a new husband picked out, and she'll strip Balfour of everything he has left when she's ready to cut loose from him."

"That's all of it?" Mason asked.

"That's all of it," she said. "Now you see why I had to get out of circulation. It was all right for a while. It looked like a hit and run. Of course, Ted was mixed up in it, but everyone knew that Ted could get a suspended sentence if he was found guilty."

"And what did you hear from Guthrie after he went to Mexico?" Mason said.

"Only this," she said, fighting to keep her lips straight as she opened her handbag and took out a crumpled wire.

She passed the wire over to Mason. Mason unfolded the yellow paper and read:

SAY NOTHING OF WHAT HAS HAPPENED. DORLA AND I HAVE REACHED FULL AGREEMENT AND BELIEVE EVERYTHING WILL COME OUT ALL RIGHT IN THE FUTURE.

GUTHRIE

"That," Mason said, "was sent from Chihuahua City?"

She nodded.

"And since that time?"

"Since that time I haven't heard a word. Dorla has been with him, and heaven knows *what* she's done."

Mason said, "Would Guthrie Balfour sit back and see Ted convicted of murder?"

"No, of course not, not of murder. He'll come forward if he has to. After all, Mr. Mason, it *was* self-defense."

"He'd have a hell of a time proving that now."

"Well, now you know the facts. What are *you* going to do?"

"There's only one thing I can do," Mason said.

"What?"

"I'm representing Ted Balfour."

"You mean you'll blow the whole case wide open?"

"I'll blow the top clean off," Mason said, "if I have to."

She looked at him with angry eyes. "I played fair with you, Mr. Mason."

"I'm playing fair with my client," Mason told her. "That's the only fair play I know."

"Do you think I'm a complete, utter fool?" she asked. "You couldn't drag that story out of me on the witness stand no matter *what* you did. I told you so you'd know, so you'd understand what to do. Can't you understand? You're working for the Balfours. They're wealthy. You can have any amount you need as a fee, only fix this thing up so that . . . well, work it out on a basis of legal technicalities so the facts never need to come out."

Mason got to his feet. "You already have my answer."

"What do you mean?" she asked.

"The paper you folded and put in your purse—your subpoena to appear as a witness on behalf of the defendant."

Chapter 15

As Perry Mason entered the office, Della Street said, "We have troubles."

"What?" Mason asked.

"I don't know. But Addison Balfour telephoned."

"Personally?"

"Personally."

"And talked with you?"

"That's right."

"What did he want?"

"He said that this wasn't the simple case it seemed, that the whole Balfour empire was threatened, that he was going to leave it up to you to work out the best deal possible. He said his right-hand man, Banner Boles, would be in touch with you within a short time, that Boles knew his way around and knew how to handle things."

"And did he say what the trouble was?"

"No."

"Or what Banner Boles wanted to see me about?"

"No. It was just to tell you that there was trouble and Boles would be seeing you."

"Okay," Mason said, "I'll see him."

"How did you come out with Florence Ingle?"

"I had a nice talk with her," Mason said.

"You don't seem very happy about it."

"I'm not."

The phone rang. Della Street answered it, said, "Yes, just a moment, Mr. Boles; I'm quite certain he'll talk with you." She cupped her hand over the mouthpiece, nodded toward the telephone, and said to Perry Mason, "This is Banner Boles on the line now."

Mason picked up the extension phone on his desk, said, "Yes, hello. This is Perry Mason talking."

"Banner Boles, Mr. Mason," a hearty voice at the other end of the line said.

"How are you, Mr. Boles?"

"Did Addison Balfour telephone you about me?"

"I understand he talked with my office," Mason said. "I'm just getting in myself."

"Well, I want to see you."

"So I understand. Come on up."

There was a moment's silence at the other end of the line, then Boles said, "This is rather a delicate matter, Mr. Mason."

"All right, we'll talk it over."

"Not in your office, I'm afraid."

"Why not?" Mason asked.

"I don't go to any man's office with the sort of stuff we're going to talk about."

"Why not?"

"How do I know it isn't bugged?"

"By me?" Mason asked.

"By anybody."

"All right," Mason said. "Where *do* you want to talk?"

"On neutral grounds," Boles said laughingly, the good nature of his voice robbing the words of any offense. "Tell you what I'll do, Mr. Mason. I'll come up to your office. As soon as I come in, you leave with me. We'll go downstairs. We'll walk as long as you suggest. Then we'll stop and take the first taxicab that comes by. We'll talk in the taxi."

"All right," Mason said. "Have it your own way."

He hung up the telephone, said to Della Street, "One of those things."

"He's coming in?"

"Coming in," Mason said. "And wants to go out where we can talk in privacy."

"Chief, I'm afraid there's a chance they'll try to frame you if you don't do what they want in this thing. These people are big and they play for keeps."

"I've had the same thought," Mason said, pacing the floor.

"You learned something from that Ingle woman, didn't you?"

"Yes."

"What?"

"Let me think it over a while," Mason said, and continued pacing the floor. Abruptly he stopped, said to Della Street, "I want to know everything there is to know about Jackson Eagan."

"But he's dead."

"I know he's dead. But I want to know everything about him. All we have is the information from his driver's license and that telegram from Paul's contact. I want to know what he looked like, where he lived, who his friends were, how it happened he died, where the body's buried, who attended the funeral. I want to know everything."

"He died in Yucatán, Mexico," Della said.

Mason said, "I want Drake to find out who identified the body. I want to find out everything about the guy, and I want a copy of that driving license of Eagan's. I want to check his thumbprint on the driver's license with that of the dead man."

Della Street nodded, went over to the typewriter, typed out a list of the things Mason wanted. The lawyer continued to pace the floor.

Della said, "I'll take this down the corridor to Paul Drake personally."

"Have one of the girls take it down," Mason said. "I want you waiting here. When Boles comes in I want you to go out and size him up before I have a talk with him."

"Okay, I'll send one of the girls down right away." Della Street went out to the outer office and was back in a moment, saying, "I sent Gertie down to Drake's office. Your man, Boles, came in while I was out there in the outer office. I told him I'd tell you he was here."

118

"What does he look like?" Mason asked.

"He's rather tall . . . oh, perhaps an inch and a half or two inches under six feet. He's very good-looking, one of those profile guys who holds his chin up high. He has black, wavy hair and very intense blue eyes. He's well dressed and has an air of assurance. You can see he's quite a diplomat."

"Yes," Mason said, "a trouble shooter for the Balfour enterprises would have to be a smart cookie.

"Let's have a look at him, Della. Is he carrying a brief-case?"

She shook her head.

"All right, tell him to come in."

Della Street went out and escorted Boles to the office. Boles came forward with a cordial smile, gripped Mason's hand in a hearty handshake, said, "I'm sorry to make a damned nuisance out of myself, Counselor, but you know how it is. Having the sort of job I do makes things rather difficult at times. Shall we take a walk?"

"Yes," Mason said, "we'll go out if you want, but I can assure you it's all right to talk here."

"No, no, let's take a walk."

"I see you're not carrying a briefcase."

Boles threw back his head and laughed. "You're a smart guy, Mason. I wouldn't pull anything as crude as that on you. I'll admit I have used a concealed tape recorder in a briefcase, but I wouldn't try it with a man of your caliber. Moreover, when I play with men like you, I play fair. I wouldn't want you to try to record my conversation and I'll be damned if I'll try to record yours."

"Fair enough," Mason said. He turned to Della Street. "Della, I'll be back about . . . hang that watch! What time is it, Boles?"

Boles instantly shot out his hand, looked at his wristwatch, said, "Ten minutes to three."

"You're way off," Mason told him.

"No, I'm not. It's exactly ten minutes to three."

"Your watch says twelve-thirty," Mason told him.

Boles laughed. "You're wrong."

"Let's take a look," Mason observed.

"I tell you you're wrong," Boles said, suddenly losing his smile.

Mason said, "I either take a look at your wristwatch, or we don't talk."

"Oh, all right," Boles said, unstrapping the wristwatch, pulling loose two wires and dropping it in his pocket. "I should have known better than to try it."

"Any other microphones?" Mason asked. "How about behind your necktie?"

"Take a look," Boles invited.

Mason felt behind the necktie, patted the inside pocket of the coat, reached inside, pulled out the small, compact wire recorder, and said, "Let's take the battery out of this and then I'll feel better."

"We'll do better than that," Boles said. "*You* carry the thing in *your* pocket. I'll keep the microphone that's made to look like a wristwatch."

"All right," Mason told him. "Let's go."

They walked silently down the corridor to the elevator, rode down the elevator to the street.

"Which way do you want to go?" Boles asked.

"Suit yourself," Mason told him.

"No, you pick the direction."

"All right. We'll go up this street here."

They walked up the street for a couple of blocks. Abruptly Mason stopped. "All right," he said, "let's catch the first cab that comes along."

They waited for two or three minutes, then found a cruising cab, climbed inside, and settled back against the cushions.

"Where to?" the driver asked.

"Straight down the street," Mason told him, "then turn out of traffic some place. We're closing this window to your compartment because we want to talk."

"Any particular destination?" the cabdriver asked.

"No. Just drive around until we tell you to turn back."

"I'm going to keep out of the traffic jams then, if you don't mind."

"Okay by us," Mason told him.

The cabdriver pushed the sliding window into place, which shut off the back of the car.

Mason turned to Boles. "All right," he said, "let's have it."

Boles said, "I'm the grease in the works of Balfour enterprises. That means I get in lots of tight spots."

Mason nodded.

"Guthrie Balfour telephoned. He wanted me to fly down and join him in Chihuahua."

Again Mason nodded.

"Now what I'm going to tell you," Boles said, "has to be absolutely confidential. You can't tell anyone anything about it."

"In talking to me," Mason said, "you are talking to a lawyer who is representing a client. I'll make no promises, bind myself to nothing."

"Remember this," Boles said ominously. "You're being paid by the Balfour enterprises."

"It doesn't make any difference who pays me," Mason said. "I'm representing a client."

Boles regarded him thoughtfully for a moment.

"Does that change the situation?" Mason asked.

"I'm going to tell you certain things," Boles said. "If you're smart, you'll play the game my way. If you try to play it any other way, you may get hurt."

"All right," Mason said. "What's the story?"

Boles said, "You're not to let Mrs. Guthrie Balfour know anything about this conversation."

"She isn't my client," Mason said, "but I make no promises."

"All right," Boles said, "here we go. You want to get some dope on Jackson Eagan, don't you?"

"I'm trying to, yes."

"Here you are," Boles said, reaching in his pocket. "Here's Jackson Eagan's driving license. Here's the carbon copy of the contract that he had with the drive-yourself car agency that rented him the automobile. Here's the receipt for the unit at the Sleepy Hollow Motel. Here's a wallet with some identification cards, some club cards and around two hundred and seventy-five dollars in currency. Here's a key ring containing a bunch of keys. Here's a very valuable wrist-watch with a broken crystal. The watch isn't running. It is stopped at one thirty-two."

Boles took the collection from his pocket, handed it across to Mason.

"What about these?" Mason asked.

"Put them in your pocket," Boles said.

Mason hesitated a moment, then dropped the assortment into his pocket. "Where did they come from?" he asked.

"Where do you think?" Boles asked.

Mason flashed a quick glance at the cabdriver, saw the driver was paying no attention to anything except the traffic ahead, then turned to Boles. "I'm listening."

"Balfour Allied Associates is a big corporation," Boles said. "The stock, however, is held entirely by members of the family. On the other hand, the members of the family have virtually no property except that stock. It's the policy of the Balfour empire to throw everything into the corporation. The members of the family draw substantial salaries. In addition to that, all of their traveling expenses, a good part of their living expenses, and many incidentals are furnished by the company under one excuse or the other, such as entertainment of customers, office rental for homework on Saturdays and Sundays and that sort of stuff."

"Go ahead," Mason said.

"You're a lawyer," Boles went on. "You can see what a setup of that kind means. If anything happened and an outsider got a judgment of any sort against one of the Balfours, an execution would be levied on the stock of the individual Balfour. In that way, unless the company made a settlement, there would be a stockholder who was an outsider. No one wants that."

"To whom are you referring?" Mason asked.

"Dorla Balfour," Boles said shortly.

"What about her?"

"Addison Balfour is the business brains of the company," Boles said. "Guthrie doesn't do very much in connection with the property management. Theodore, who was Ted Balfour's father, was pretty much of a right-hand man for Addison, but Guthrie is a total loss as far as the business is concerned.

"Naturally, when Guthrie remarried and picked up a girl like Dorla, Addison regarded the entire transaction with considerable consternation. He attended the wedding, offered his congratulations, kissed the bride, then very quietly started building up a slush fund in the form of cash which he could use to make a property settlement with Dorla when the time came."

"Go on," Mason said.

"However," Boles said, "Dorla couldn't even wait to play the game cleverly. She started playing around. I won't go into details. Naturally, Addison, while he had hardly dared hope for this, was prepared for it. He told me to keep an eye on her.

"I was ready to get the goods on her which would have taken Guthrie off the hook, when Guthrie somehow or other became suspicious and like a damn fool tried to pick up his own evidence.

"If he'd only come to me, I could have shown him photostats of motel registers where she and this Jackson Eagan had registered together dozens of times.

"However, Guthrie wanted to get the evidence his own way. He was going to be smart—the damn fool!

"Guthrie started out on this trip to Mexico. He told Dorla he wanted her to ride on the train as far as the Pasadena-Alhambra station. That was so she'd know that he was on the train and would get careless."

"It worked?" Mason asked, his voice carefully masked.

"Admirably. She got off one side of the train; Guthrie opened a vestibule door on the other side of the train, dropped off on the blind side, waited until the train had pulled out, walked over to the car that he had rented, and followed Dorla.

"Dorla was in a hurry. She couldn't wait to get to the Sleepy Hollow Motel, where this steady boyfriend, Jackson Eagan, was registered. She went in with him, there was an ardent reunion, and then after a while Dorla came out. She went home to get some things.

"Guthrie had come prepared for all eventualities. But as it happened, fate played into his hands. The motel unit next to the one occupied by Jackson was empty. Guthrie had a tape recorder with a very sensitive microphone that fastens up against the wall. He put the mike up against the wall and settled back to listen.

"That microphone picked up sounds which were inaudible to the ear, but he could plug a pair of earphones in and listen as the tape went over a secondary head, which enabled him to listen to everything that was on the tape."

Mason nodded again.

"He listened to plenty," Boles said. "Then Dorla left in Jackson Eagan's car to get her suitcase.

"Well, that's when Guthrie Balfour did the most foolish thing of all.

"He had all the evidence he needed on the tape recorder. But, like a bungling amateur, he thought he could confront Jackson Eagan, take the part of the outraged husband, and get Eagan to sign some sort of a confession.

"So Guthrie opened the door and went into the dimly lit motel. Eagan aimed a flashlight at his face, recognized him and they started fighting. Guthrie had the .22 automatic he had taken from the glove compartment of Ted's car. There was a struggle. The gun went off and Eagan fell to the floor with a bullet in his head.

"Guthrie got in a panic. He dashed out of the place and

124

ran to the telephone booth that was in front of the office. He called the trouble number. That's where I came in.

"That telephone has right of way over anything. I answered the phone. Guthrie told me he was at the Sleepy Hollow Motel, that he'd had trouble and that it was *very* serious.

"I told him to wait and I'd get out there right away. Guthrie was scared stiff. He could hardly talk on the phone. He seemed to be in pretty much of a daze.

"I got out there in nothing flat. Guthrie was seated in his rented car and was shaking like a leaf. I finally got out of him what had happened."

"So what did you do?" Mason asked.

"I did the only thing there was to do," Boles said. "Guthrie was supposed to be on a train to El Paso, en route to Chihuahua. Nobody knew he'd gotten off that train. I told him to take the company plane, fly to Phoenix, and get aboard the train. I told him that I'd arrange to come down later on and pick up the plane. I told him I'd take care of everything and not to bother."

"So what did he do?"

"Started off to get the plane, just as I told him."

"He could fly it himself?"

"Sure, he could fly it himself. He had a key to the hangar. He takes off from a private landing field at the suburban factory. There was absolutely nothing to stand in his way. It was a cinch."

"What did you do?"

"What do you think I did?" Boles asked. "I took the body out. I tied it on my car and dragged the face off it. I banged it around so the head was smashed up like an eggshell, took it out and dumped it on the highway, so it would look like a hit and run. Fortunately, the gun was a small-caliber gun, there hadn't been any hemorrhage, and what bleeding had taken place had been on the rug in the motel unit. I took that rug, put it in the car, and subsequently burned it up. I took the rug out of the unit Balfour had been occupying and put it in the unit Eagan had occupied.

"Before I'd got very far with what I was doing, Dorla came back."

"What did you tell her?"

"I did what any good trouble shooter should have done under the circumstances," Boles said. "I told her that I'd been the one who was shadowing her, that I knew all about what she was doing, that I had the dope on her, that I had a tape recording that showed her guilty of infidelity. I told her that I had a written statement from Jackson Eagan, but that after I got the written statement out of him he jumped me and I had to shoot him in self-defense.

"I told Dorla to help me plant the body and make it look like a hit and run and then that she was to take the first plane to Tucson, and get aboard the train Guthrie was on. She was to tell Guthrie she was in a jam, that she'd been driving while intoxicated and had hit a man with a family car, that it was up to him to protect her, that he was to swear he'd talked her into staying on the train with him, and that she'd been on the train all the time. He was to take her down to Mexico with him and he was to give her an alibi.

"In that way, I had Dorla mixed into the thing up to her pretty little eyebrows. I had her really believing that Guthrie had been on the train all the time and that *I* was the only one who knew anything about what had been going on."

"Then she helped you get the car Ted had been driving?" Mason asked.

"Sure. We planted the guy in the right place and then I had Dorla wait until after Ted came home with the car. Fortunately he was pretty pie-eyed. Marilyn Keith took him upstairs and, I guess, put him to bed. Then she came down, and I'll sure hand it to that kid! She was plucky. She didn't even leave a back trail by calling for a taxicab. She walked out to State Highway and took a chance on hitchhiking a ride home. For an attractive girl like that, that was quite some chance. That's a lot of devotion to her job. I'm going to see

126

that that girl gets a real raise in pay as soon as this thing is over."

"Go on," Mason said. "Then what happened?"

"After that, it was all just a matter of cleaning up details," Boles said. "Dorla took the car out, smashed into the guy. We left a few clues scattered around. Then she took the car back and parked it. I called the cops next morning and gave them an anonymous tip on the Balfour car.

"Now that's where Dorla double-crossed me. She's a smart little trollop. I had it planned so the evidence would point to *her* as the one who had driven the car and hit the man.

"She played it smart. Before she took the plane to Tucson, she sneaked into Ted's room and planted the car key in Ted's pocket. Ted was dead to the world. The Keith girl had left him with all his clothes on except his shoes. She'd taken those off. Dorla undressed him, put his pajamas on, and fixed it so he thought he'd gone out a second time and that the accident probably had happened then.

"Now then, Mason, that gives you an idea what you're up against."

"One other question," Mason said. "What about the witness, Myrtle Anne Haley?"

"A complete phony," Boles said. "I had a body to account for and we wanted to be certain that Dorla was where she could be charged with the hit and run—unless she got Guthrie to back her on her fake alibi. That would put Dorla completely in our power. But the time element became confused, Ted talked too much to the investigating officers, and Dorla did too good a job getting Guthrie to back up her phony alibi. So that left Ted holding the bag. I hadn't planned it that way but Ted *shouldn't* have had any trouble beating the case. Then that damn fool, Howland, loused everything up.

"I got this witness, this Myrtle Anne Haley who is working for the Balfour enterprises. I told her what she had to swear to— The dumb cluck got it pretty well mixed up. I've used her before. She's loyal, even if she isn't smart. For a thousand bucks she'll play along with anything.

127

"I admit I made a mistake with Howland. I didn't pay him by the day. I paid him by the job. So Howland saw an opportunity to wipe it all off the books by making a deal with the prosecution under which Ted would get a suspended sentence.

"Now then, there's the story. I've dumped it in your lap."

"What do you expect *me* to do with it?" Mason asked.

"You've made a good start already," Boles said. "That's one hell of a clever point you made with that once-in-jeopardy business. You go ahead and pull that prior conviction stuff for all it's worth. Never let them get to trial on the merits. Keep hammering home that point of being once in jeopardy. I think it's a hell of a good point. So does a lawyer whom I've consulted. He says you're tops and you've got a point there that will keep them from ever bringing out the evidence they have. He says you're a genius."

"I may not be able to work it that way," Mason said coldly.

"What do you mean?"

"Suppose I put in a plea of once in jeopardy and the judge overrules it? Then the district attorney goes to trial."

"Exactly," Boles said. "And at that time you don't take any part in the trial at all. You simply sit back and let them handle it all their own way. You refuse to cross-examine witnesses. You refuse to put on any witnesses of your own. You refuse to argue anything except this plea of once in jeopardy. Then, if the jury returns a verdict of guilty, you're in a position to go before the Supreme Court on that once-in-jeopardy point. You will have aroused the sympathy of the Supreme Court because you didn't put on any evidence and didn't make any defense."

"Are you," Mason asked, "telling me how to conduct the case?"

There was a moment's silence. Boles' blue eyes became hard as steel. "You're damn right I am. We're paying the bill."

"You may be paying the bill," Mason told him, "but I'm

representing a client. Suppose the Supreme Court doesn't set aside the verdict on my once-in-jeopardy theory? Then young Balfour is convicted of murder.''

"A damn sight better to have Ted Balfour convicted of second-degree murder than to have the whole Balfour family rocked by a family scandal and a verdict of first-degree murder. Ted isn't important. Guthrie Balfour is. However, we could easily make out a case of self-defense for Ted where we couldn't for Guthrie.''

Mason said, "My responsibility is to my client.''

"Look," Boles said coldly, "your obligation is to do what I tell you to do. We're paying the freight. I'm master-minding this thing. You try to double-cross me and I'll make you the sickest individual in the state of California. And don't ever forget I can do it.

"You're supposed to be smart and to know your way around. If you had half of the things to contend with that I've had to take in my stride, you'd realize you didn't know anything. Don't think this is the first killing I've had to square. And some of the things have been pretty damn nasty.''

"All right," Mason said. "Now I know your position and you know mine. I'll also tell you something to remember: I don't suborn perjury and I don't go for all this crooked business. I rely on the truth. The truth is a better weapon than all these crooked schemes of yours.''

Boles said, "You're kicking a chance at a hundred-thousand-dollar fee out the window and you're leaving yourself wide open.''

"To hell with the fee," Mason said. "I'm protecting my client. I'll do what I think is for his best interests.''

Boles reached forward and tapped on the window of the cab.

The driver turned around.

"Stop right here. Let me out," Boles said.

Boles turned to Mason. "Under the circumstances, you can pay for the cab.''

Mason whipped a paper from his pocket and shoved it in Boles' hand as the cab lurched to a stop.

"What's this?" Boles asked.

"A subpoena ordering you to attend court as a witness for the defense," Mason said.

For a moment Boles' jaw sagged open in incredulous surprise, then he said, "Why you dirty son-of-a-bitch!"

Boles slammed the car door shut with a vigor which rattled the glass.

"Turn around," Mason instructed the cabdriver. "Go back to the place where you picked us up."

Chapter 16

Perry Mason regarded the letter which Della Street placed on his desk on top of the morning mail.

"You say that came registered mail, special delivery?"

She nodded. "They don't lose any time, do they?"

Mason read aloud:

"Dear Sir:

"You are hereby notified that, effective immediately, you are relieved of all duties in connection with the defense of Theodore Balfour, Jr., in the case of People versus Balfour. From now on the defendant will be represented by Mortimer Dean Howland as his attorney. You will please submit any expenses which you have incurred to date, together with the necessary vouchers showing the nature and extent of those expenses. From the date of receipt of this communication, you will incur no more expenses on behalf of the Balfour Allied Associates, and any such bills as you may submit for your personal compensation to date in connection with said case will be predicated upon a per diem basis. Otherwise, those bills will be contested. We will allow you a maximum of two hundred and fifty dollars per day for your time.

"Very truly yours,

"BALFOUR ALLIED ASSOCIATES
"per Addison Balfour

"Makes it nice and official, doesn't it?" Mason said.

"What about Ted Balfour? Do you have to withdraw simply because—"

"Not because Addison Balfour says so," Mason observed. "But put yourself in Ted's place. Boles goes to him ad tells him that I won't cooperate and that the Balfour Allied Associates have lost confidence in me, that they're not putting up any more money for his defense as long as I'm connected with the case in any way, that if Mortimer Dean Howland represents him they will go the limit. What would *you* do under those circumstances?"

"Well, what are you going to do?"

"I'm damned if I know," Mason said thoughtfully. "If I go to young Balfour and tell him the truth, Howland will claim that I'm guilty of unprofessional conduct in trying to solicit employment.

"The probabilities are that if I even try to see Balfour, I'll be advised that Balfour has stated I am no longer representing him and therefore I have no visitor's privileges."

"So what are you going to do?"

"So," Mason said, "I'm going to put it up to Ted Balfour. At least, I'm going to try to see him."

"And what are you going to tell him?"

"I'm going to shoot the works."

The telephone on Della Street's desk rang. She picked it up, said, "Just a minute," turned to Mason and said, "Your first client is back. Marilyn Keith. Says she has to see you at once on a matter of the greatest urgency."

"Show her in," Mason said.

Marilyn Keith had quite evidently been crying, but her chin was high and she didn't try to avoid Mason's probing eyes.

Her quick eyes flashed at the pile of mail on Mason's desk. "I see you received your notification," she said.

Mason nodded.

She said, "Mr. Mason, I'm sorry that you had a difference of opinion with Banner Boles. He's . . . well, he's very, very powerful and he's very, very clever."

Mason merely nodded.

"I know, of course, what it's all about," she said, indicating the notification on the desk. "Mr. Addison Balfour dictated that to me and had me take it to the main post office, so that you'd get it first thing this morning."

Mason said, "Let's be frank, Miss Keith. You're working for the Balfour Allied Associates. A situation has developed where the interests of Ted Balfour may have become adverse to those of your employer. I don't want you to—"

"Oh, forget it!" she blazed. "Don't be so damn stupid!"

Mason raised his eyebrows.

"For your official information," she said, "I am no longer employed by the Balfour Allied Associates."

"What happened?"

She said, "I have been accused of betraying my employer, of being disloyal, and of using confidential information which I received in the course of my employment for my personal advantage."

"Mind telling what happened?" Mason asked, the lines of his face softening somewhat. "And do sit down. I only have a minute, but I'm anxious to hear what you have to say."

She said, "I went up to the jail to call on Ted Balfour."

"You did!" Mason exclaimed.

She nodded.

"And what did you tell him?"

"I told him that the Balfour Allied Associates were cutting off all their aid as long as he had you for a lawyer, that if he accepted Mortimer Dean Howland as his lawyer and discharged you, the Balfour Allied Associates would put up all of the money that was necessary to fight his case all the way through the courts on the theory that you had raised; to wit, that he had once been placed in jeopardy and therefore couldn't be tried again.

"I also told him that, while I didn't know the details, I knew that the Balfour Allied Associates were prepared to toss him to the wolves in order to save their own skins. I told him that if he insisted on keeping you as his attorney, I was satisfied that you would loyally represent his interests to the best of your ability."

"And what did he do?"

"Well," she said, "he wanted to keep you if there was any way of paying you."

"He told you that?"

"Yes."

"So what did you do?"

She opened her purse, said, "I made out a check to you in an amount of five hundred and twenty-five dollars. That's every cent I have in the world, Mr. Mason, and I don't know when you're going to get any more. I know that's not the type of fee you get in a murder case. It's just on account."

Mason took the check, studied it for a moment.

"I'll get another job somewhere," she said bravely, "and I'll set aside a regular percentage of my paycheck. I'll give you a promissory note, Mr. Mason, and—"

Mason said, "You're not likely to get another job with the Balfour Allied Associates making charges that you used confidential information for your own personal gain."

She fought back tears. "I'm not foolish enough to try it here," she said. "I'm going to some other city and I'm not going to tell them anything about having been with Balfour Allied Associates."

Mason stood thoughtfully regarding her.

"Will you do it, Mr. Mason? Will you, *please*? Oh, will you *please* represent Ted?"

"He wants me to?" Mason asked.

"Very much," she said. "It's an uphill battle, but you'll be honest. And you'll have a terrific fight. You have no idea of the ruthless power of the Balfour Allied Associates, or the manner in which Banner Boles uses that power.

"Boles was educated as an attorney, although he never practiced. He's been a lobbyist and he knows his way around. You give that man unlimited money and all the power of the Balfour Allied Associates back of him, and anything that he can't buy out of his way he'll club out of his way."

"Do you think Ted will want me after Boles has been to see him?"

"That's why I had to see you now," she said. "You go and see Ted. Go and see him right now. Tell him that you're going to stay with him. But please, Mr. Mason, please don't tell him that *I* am paying anything. Oh, I know it's pitifully inadequate. But if you only can . . . if you only will . . ."

Mason picked up her check, tore it in half, tore the halves into quarters, dropped the pieces in the wastebasket, walked over and put his arm around her shoulder. "You poor kid," he said. "Forget it. I'll go and see Ted Balfour and tell him that I'll stand by him. You save your money for a cushion until you can get another job. You'll need it."

She looked up at him for a moment, then lost all semblance of maintaining her poise. Her head came forward on the lawyer's shoulder and her body was shaken by sobs.

Della Street tactfully eased out of the room.

Chapter 17

Judge Cadwell said, "Gentlemen, the jury has been sworn. The defendant is in court. The jurors are all present.

"I may state that, while I do not consider myself prejudiced so that I am disqualified from trying the issues in this case, I was hoping that it would be assigned to another judge. I have, of course, already become familiar with the legal point raised by the defense in connection with habeas corpus.

"It appears that the facts supporting the plea of once in jeopardy are completely within the knowledge of the Court. There is no dispute as to those facts. There is therefore no issue to go to the jury in connection with a plea of once in jeopardy. It becomes a matter for the Court to pass upon as a matter of law. The Court therefore decides that there is no merit to the plea of once in jeopardy.

"The Court makes this ruling with some hesitancy because it is aware that the point is a close one. However, this Court simply can't conceive that it is the purpose of the law to clothe a defendant with immunity simply because, through a misinterpretation of facts or a paucity of facts, prosecution was originally had upon another theory, or for a lesser offense. Yet the Court is forced to admit that the authorities seem to indicate such is the case.

"In view of the undisputed facts in the case the point is one which can be taken to the appellate courts and passed upon by them. Therefore, the real interests of the defendant will in no wise be curtailed by this ruling of the Court. I overrule the plea of once in jeopardy and the prosecution will proceed with its case."

Roger Farris made a brief opening statement to the jury and then started putting on witnesses.

The autopsy surgeon in the coroner's office testified to having performed an autopsy on a body which had at first been certified out as a hit-and-run case. Afterwards, the body had been exhumed when it appeared that there were certain discrepancies in the evidence. At that time a more detailed examination of the skull had been made, and it was found that death had resulted from a bullet wound. The course and nature of the bullet wound was described and the bullet, which had been recovered from the wound, was introduced in evidence.

Mason offered no questions on cross-examination.

A .22 automatic was produced and identified by manufacturer's number. The sales record showed that the weapon had been sold to the defendant Ted Balfour.

Again there was no cross-examination.

Roger Farris put a witness on the stand who qualified as an expert on firearms and firearms identification. He testified that he had fired test bullets from the automatic and had compared them with the fatal bullet which had been introduced in evidence, and that the markings on the bullet showed beyond doubt that the fatal bullet had been fired from the automatic which had been received in evidence.

Again Mason did not cross-examine.

Judge Cadwell frowned down at Mason. "Now let me understand the position of counsel," he said. "Is it the position of counsel that, because the Court has overruled the plea of once in jeopardy, counsel intends to take no part in this trial? Because, if such is to be the position of counsel, I feel that the Court should warn counsel that counsel is here for the purpose of representing the interests of the defendant, and that, as an officer of the Court, it is the duty of counsel to see that the defendant is represented."

"I understand the Court's position," Mason said. "I am not cross-examining these witnesses, because I have no ques-

137

tions to ask of them. I intend to participate actively in this trial.''

"Very well,'' Judge Cadwell said frowning. "The Court needs only to point out, Mr. Mason, the importance of these witnesses. However, the Court will make no comment on the testimony. Proceed with the case.''

"Now then, Your Honor,'' Roger Farris said, "it appears that Myrtle Anne Haley, who was a witness for the People at the previous trial of this action when the defendant was indicted for negligent homicide, is at the moment unavailable. We propose to show that we have made every effort to locate her. Being unable to do so, in view of the fact that the parties to this action are the same as the parties in the other action, to wit, the People of the State of California as plaintiff and Theodore Balfour, Jr., as defendant, we wish to read her testimony into the record. I understand there is no objection.''

"Any objection?'' Judge Cadwell asked.

Mason smiled. "Not in the least, Your Honor. I am glad to have this done if counsel will first prove the witness is unavailable. This action on the part of counsel, using the identical evidence used in the other trial shows the solidity of our plea of once in jeopardy.''

"The actions aren't the same,'' Farris said. "The parties are the same, that's all.''

Judge Cadwell stroked his chin. "Of course,'' he said, "that does tend to give force to the defendant's plea of once in jeopardy. However, the Court has ruled on that, and that ruling will stand. Make your showing, Mr. Prosecutor. Counsel will be advised that any objection which counsel wishes to take to any question as contained in the transcript may be made at this time and the Court will then rule on that objection.''

Farris produced an investigator for the district attorney's office who testified that Myrtle Anne Haley had moved from her residence and had left no forwarding address, that he had talked with all of her friends and acquaintances but no one

138

knew where she had gone, that he had made every effort to find her and serve a subpoena on her without avail. She had been employed by a subsidiary of the Balfour Allied Associates and she had left abruptly without even calling for her last paycheck. The intimation was strongly that pressure brought to bear by the Balfour company had caused this prime witness for the prosecution to absent herself.

"Cross-examination?" Judge Cadwell asked Mason.

Mason shook his head. "No cross-examination."

"Very well," Judge Cadwell said, "I will grant the motion of the prosecution that the testimony of Myrtle Anne Haley may be read in the record, after that testimony is properly authenticated, there being no objection."

The court reporter was thereupon duly sworn and read the transcript of Myrtle Anne Haley's testimony.

With the manner of a magician bringing a startling trick to a breath-taking conclusion, Roger Farris called out in a ringing voice, "Will Mr. Banner Boles take the stand?"

Banner Boles came forward, held up his hand, was sworn, gave his name, age, residence, and occupation, and settled himself comfortably in the witness stand.

"Are you acquainted with the defendant, Theodore Balfour, Jr.?" Farris asked.

"Yes, sir. Certainly."

"How long have you known him?"

"For some ten years."

"What were you doing on the nineteenth of September of this year?"

"I was working for the Balfour Allied Associates."

"Specifically what duties did you perform that night?"

"Mr. Guthrie Balfour was leaving for El Paso. From there he was going to Mexico. It was part of my assignment to see that he got safely aboard the train."

"Somewhat in the nature of a bodyguard?"

"Well, more in the nature of a general trouble shooter."

"You saw him on the train for El Paso?"

"I did."

"Who else?"

"His wife, Dorla Balfour."

"She boarded the same train with him?"

"Yes, sir."

"Where had you been prior to the time you went to the depot?"

"There had been a little social gathering, something in the nature of a going-away party at the home of Mrs. Florence Ingle who is a friend of the Balfours."

"And you had been at that party?"

"I had, yes, sir."

"And what happened after you escorted Mr. and Mrs. Guthrie Balfour to the train?"

"I went back to my office."

"You have an office uptown?"

"Yes, sir."

"It is not at the Balfour Allied Associates?"

"I have an office there too, but I have an uptown office which is kept open twenty-four hours a day."

"For what purpose, may I ask?"

"People call me when something comes up and there is any trouble."

"And were you called on the evening of the nineteenth?"

"No, sir."

"You were not?"

"No, sir."

"I thought— Oh, I beg your pardon, it was early in the morning of the twentieth. Were you called then?"

"Yes, sir."

"Who called you?"

"The defendant."

"You are referring to the defendant, Theodore Balfour, Jr.?"

"Yes, sir."

"Do you know where he was calling you from?"

"I only know where he said he was calling me from."

"And where was that?"

140

"It was a telephone booth at a service station at the intersection of Sycamore Road and State Highway. The service station was closed but he was calling from the booth."

"And what did he say?"

"He asked me to join him at once. He said he was in trouble."

"What did you do?"

"I jumped in my car and got out there as quick as I could."

"How long did it take?"

"About twenty minutes, I guess."

"Did you give the defendant any instructions before you left?"

"I told him to wait there until I arrived."

"Was he there when you arrived?"

"No, sir. He was not."

"Where was he?"

"Well, I cruised around for a while trying to find—"

"Never mind that. Tell us where you finally found the defendant."

"I found him at home."

"That is, at the residence of Mr. and Mrs. Guthrie Balfour?"

"Yes, sir."

"That was where he was living?"

"Yes, sir."

"As a trouble shooter for the Balfour Allied Associates you knew that, did you?"

"Yes, sir."

"And what did you do?"

"I didn't want to get everybody up. I wanted to find out if the defendant was home."

"In your capacity with the organization, do you have keys for the residences of the executives of the Balfour Allied Associates?"

"I have pass keys I can use if there is an emergency."

"And did you use one of those keys?"

"Yes, sir."

"Where did you go first?"

"First I looked in the garage to see if the car the defendant had been driving was in the garage."

"You found that it was in the garage?"

"Yes, sir."

"What was its condition?"

"Well, I used my flashlight and walked around the car looking for signs of trouble because from the tone of voice in which the defendant had telephoned me, I thought he had been—"

"Never mind what you *thought*," Farris interrupted sharply. "Just tell what you *did*."

"I looked the car over."

"What did you find?"

"I found that the right front headlight was smashed, that there was a dent in the right fender, and there were a few flecks of blood on the front bumper near the right-hand side; that is, I assumed the spots were blood. They were red spots which had crusted and looked like blood."

"So then what did you do?"

"So then I switched off my flashlight, closed the garage door, went to the house, inserted my key in the front door, opened the front door, and walked upstairs."

"And where did you go?"

"To the room occupied by the defendant."

"You had been in that room before?"

"Oh, yes."

"You knew where it was?"

"Yes, sir."

"And what did you do?"

"I tapped on the door and said, 'This is Banner, Ted. Let me in.' "

"Did you receive any response?"

"No, sir."

"What did you do?"

"I went inside the room."

"And what did you find?"

"I found the defendant very drunk, in what I would call and alcoholic stupor, lying fully clothed on the bed."

"What about his shoes? Were they on or off?"

"They were on."

"What time was this?"

"This was about two o'clock in the morning. I had left the service station at one-fifty, and I guess it took me about five minutes to look through the garage and study the automobile."

"Now, when you say, 'the automobile,' what automobile do you mean?"

"I mean the automobile photographs of which have been introduced in evidence, the one having license number GMB 665."

"Did you have any conversation with the defendant there in his room at that time?"

"Yes, sir."

"Who else was present?"

"No one."

"Just the two of you?"

"Yes, sir."

"What did you do?"

"I had quite a time getting the defendant so he could wake up and talk."

"What did you do?"

"I took off his coat. I took off his overshirt. I took off his undershirt. I got towels, soaked them in cold water, and put them on his abdomen and on his neck. I sat him up in bed and shook him. I put cold compresses on his eyes and on the back of his neck, and finally he became conscious, or wakened, or whatever you want to call it."

"He recognized you?"

"Oh, yes."

"And what was the conversation you had with him at that time as nearly as you can remember?"

"Well, I asked him what he wanted, and he told me he

had been in a jam but he had finally figured how to get out of it all by himself.''

''What did he tell you?''

''He told me that he had been gambling at cards pretty heavy, that he had run out of cash and had been using the credit that he had with a certain syndicate, that he had sustained losses and that those losses had piled up and the syndicate had called on him to pay.''

''He told you all this?''

''Yes, sir.''

''How did he speak?''

''His voice was thick. He was quite intoxicated, but I got it out of him a bit at a time.''

''Go ahead. Then what did he tell you?''

''He told me that he had received a couple of telephone calls from the syndicate saying he had to pay up or else. After that he said he had received an anonymous, unsigned letter saying that if he didn't pay up they were going to send their 'collector.' ''

''Did he tell you what he thought the threat meant when they said that they were going to send their collector?''

''Yes, sir.''

''What did he say?''

''He said that that meant someone to beat him up. He said that they got pretty tough with fellows that didn't pay, that the first time they beat them up, and the second time they took them for a one-way ride.''

''Go on,'' Farris said, glancing triumphantly at the jurors who were sitting on the edges of their chairs, leaning forward, drinking in Boles' words with rapt attention. ''What else did he say?''

''Well, he said that he had tried to raise twenty thousand dollars, that he didn't dare to go to Addison Balfour, that he had hoped an opportunity would present itself to speak to Guthrie Balfour before he took off for Mexico, but that, in the crush of the party, there had been no opportunity. He
144

knew that he would have to approach the subject very tactfully. Otherwise, he would be rebuffed.

"He stated that he had some money that was in a trust fund which had been left him by his parents, and that he had been trying to reach the trustee in order to get some money from him, but that the trustee was out of town on a vacation, that he was hoping he could stall the matter along until the return of the trustee."

"Did he say anything else?"

"He said that he had talked to one of his father's friends, a Florence Ingle."

"That was the woman who had given the party?"

"Yes."

"Did he say when he had talked with her?"

"He said that night. He said that he had asked her for twenty thousand dollars but that she had been unable or unwilling to give it to him."

"Then what did he say?"

"He said that he drank more than was good for him, that he was rather intoxicated by somewhere around ten o'clock, that a young woman had driven his car home for him, and had put the car in the garage."

"Did he tell you the name of the young woman?"

"He *said* that he didn't know the young woman's identity. But I thought he did. However, I didn't—"

"Never mind what you *thought*!" Farris shouted. "You're familiar with the rules of examination, Mr. Boles. Kindly refrain from giving any of your conclusions. Tell us only what the defendant said to you and what you said to the defendant."

"Yes, sir."

"Now, what did the defendant say to you about having been brought home?"

"Well, the defendant said he had been brought home by this young woman, that she had taken his shoes off, that he had stretched out on the bed, that he had been pretty drunk and that he had gone to the bathroom and been sick, that

145

after that he felt a little better. He suddenly remembered that the trustee who handled his trust fund sometimes came back early from a vacation, and checked in at a motel on the outskirts of town, that this man was an elderly man with poor eyesight who disliked to drive at night, and that, when he returned from a trip and it was late, he would stay at a motel on the outskirts of town rather than drive in. He said he decided to drive out and see if the trustee had returned.''

"And then what?"

"So he put on his shoes, let himself out of the house, and went to the garage. He said, however, that because of the threats which had been made and because of the late hour, he had opened his gun cabinet and had taken a .22 automatic which he had put in his pocket.''

"Go on. What else did he say?"

"He said that, when he reached the garage, he thought he saw a shadowy figure; that, because he had been drinking, he finally decided it was just his imagination; that he opened the garage door and stepped inside; and that, just as he had his hand on the handle of the car door, someone put his hand on his shoulder from behind and said, 'Okay, buddy, I'm the collector.' ''

"Go on," Farris said. "What else?"

"He said he was frozen with terror for the moment and that then the man who had said he was a collector hit him a hard blow in the chest, a blow that slammed him back against the wall of the garage; that the man had then said, 'That's a sample! Now get in the car. You and I are going for a little ride. I'm going to teach you not to welch on bets.' ''

"Go on," Farris said. "What else?"

"And then the defendant told me that almost without thinking and in actual fear of his life he had jerked out the .22 automatic and had fired from the hip; that he was an exceptionally good shot; and that he had shot directly at the man's head. The man staggered back, half-sprawled against the front seat. He was not dead, but was unconscious.

"The defendant said that he knew he had to do something

146

at once; that he had lifted this man into the front seat of the automobile; that he closed the car door; that he jumped in the other side, and drove, anxious only to get away from the house for fear that someone might have heard the shot. He said he drove down to the State Highway; that he turned left and stopped at the closed service station on Sycamore; that he called me from the phone booth there and asked me to come at once. He wanted me to tell him what could be done and how he could arrange for medical attention for the man in the car.

"He then told me that after he had hung up and returned to the car, he discovered the man was no longer breathing; that he put his hand on his wrist and there was no pulse; that the man had died while he was telephoning.

"He said that changed the situation materially; that he had then tried to call me again, but that my assistant who answered the telephone assured him I had already left."

"Go on," Farris said, "what else did he tell you? Did he tell you what he did after that?"

"Yes, sir."

"What was it?"

"He said that he felt that the problem was simplified because he had only a dead man to deal with. He said that the shock had sobered him up pretty much, that he searched the body and took everything in the line of papers that the man might have—all means of identification; that he took the man's wallet; that he even took his handkerchief, so it would not be possible to trace a laundry mark; that he took his key ring, his pocketknife, all of his personal belongings."

"Then what?"

"He said that he ran the car out Sycamore Road and then got out and placed the body on the front bumper; that he drove as fast as he could and then suddenly slammed on the brakes; that the body rolled off the bumper and skidded and rolled for some considerable distance along the highway; that he then deliberately ran over the head, then turned the car around and ran over the head again; that he ran over the head

147

several times, so as to be sure that not only would the features be unrecognizable but that it would prevent the bullet hole from showing.''

"Did he tell you anything about a bullet being in the head?''

"He told me that he thought the bullet had gone clean through the head and was in the garage somewhere.''

"Go on," Farris said.

"Well, the defendant asked me to take charge of things from there on. I told him that there was nothing much I could do; that he had already done everything; that I felt the best thing to do was to go and find the body and report the matter to the police, stating that he had acted in self-defense and in fear of his life; that this man had assaulted him first.''

"So what was done?''

"I told him to wait there, that I would go and find the body. He described exactly where he had left it.''

"And what happened?''

"I found I was too late. By the time I got there a police car was there and I felt that, under the circumstances, I didn't want to assume the responsibility of notifying the police. I thought that I would wait until I had an opportunity to think the matter over.''

"To discuss the matter with your superiors?'' Farris said sharply.

"Well, I wanted time to think it over.''

"You realized that you should have reported this?''

"Yes, sir.''

"And you didn't do so?''

"No, sir.''

"Why?''

"Because I am paid to see that matters are handled smoothly. I didn't want to hush this thing up. I wanted to see one of my friends on the police force and see if I could find some way of making a report that would not be publicized. I knew that if I reported to the police officers who were there with the body, there would be publicity, that the defendant would be picked up and lodged in jail, and I felt that—well, I felt that wasn't the best way for a trouble shooter to handle an affair of that sort."

"So what did you finally do?"

"I went back and helped Ted Balfour get undressed and into his pajamas. He wanted some more to drink and I didn't stop him in the least. In fact, I encouraged him to drink, hoping that he might forget about the whole business."

"And then?"

"And then I took from him the papers he had taken from the body and went home and went to bed."

"And then?" Farris asked.

"And then I slept late the next morning. When I awakened I learned that police had already interrogated the defendant; that in some way they had learned his automobile had been involved in the matter; and that he was going to be prosecuted for an involuntary homicide with a car."

"So what did you do?"

"I did nothing."

Farris, with the manner of a television director who has brought his show to a conclusion right on the exact second, looked up at the clock and said, "Your Honor, it seems to be the hour for the noon adjournment. While I think I have now concluded my direct examination of this witness, it might be well to have the noon recess at this time, because I would like to go over the testimony in my mind and see if perhaps I have left out a question."

"Just a minute," the judge said. "The Court has one question before we adjourn. Mr. Boles, you have stated you took those papers from the defendant?"

"Yes, sir."

"What did you do with them?"

"I held them for a while."

"Where are they now?"

"To the best of my knowledge, they are in the possession of Mr. Perry Mason."

"What?" Judge Cadwell exclaimed, coming bolt upright on the bench.

"Yes, Your Honor."

"You gave those papers to Perry Mason?"

"Yes, sir."

"Has Mr. Mason communicated with the district attorney's office in any way concerning those papers?" Judge Cadwell asked Roger Farris.

"No, Your Honor."

"When did you give Mr. Mason those papers?" Judge Cadwell asked.

"I don't have the exact date. I gave them to him after he had become associated, that is, after he had taken over the defense of Ted Balfour. During the first case the attorney representing the defendant was Mortimer Dean Howland."

"You said nothing to Mr. Howland about those papers?"

"No, sir."

"Did you say anything to anyone at any time about having those papers other than to Mr. Mason?"

"No, sir."

"And you gave those papers to Mr. Mason?"

"Yes, sir."

"Mr. Mason!" Judge Cadwell said.

"Yes, Your Honor."

"The Court . . ." Judge Cadwell's voice trailed off into silence. "The Court is about to take the noon recess," he said. "Immediately after the discharge of the jury, I would like to have counsel for both sides approach the bench. The Court will admonish the jury not to form or express any opinion in this case until it is finally submitted to the jury for decision. The jurors will not discuss the case with others or permit it to be discussed in their presence. Court will now take a recess until two o'clock.

"Mr. Mason and Mr. Farris, will you please come forward?"

Mason and Farris approached the bench, Farris trying to keep his face in a mask of grave, judicial concern as befitted one who is called upon to be present at a time when a brother attorney is subjected to a tongue lashing. Judge Cadwell waited until the jurors had filed from the courtroom. Then he said, "Mr. Mason, is this true?"

"I doubt it, Your Honor," Mason said.

"You what?" Judge Cadwell snapped.

"I doubt it."

"I mean about the papers."

"Some papers were given to me, yes."

"By Mr. Boles?"

"Yes, Your Honor."

"And did he tell you those were papers that he had taken from the defendant or that had been given him by the defendant?"

"No, sir."

"What were those papers?"

"I have them here, Your Honor."

Mason produced a sealed Manila envelope and handed it to the judge.

Judge Cadwell ripped open the envelope, started looking through the papers.

"Mr. Mason," he said, "this is a very grave matter."

"Yes, Your Honor."

"The papers in this envelope are matters of evidence. They constitute most important bits of evidence in the case."

"Evidence of what?" Mason asked.

"Evidence corroborating Boles' story, for one thing," Judge Cadwell snapped.

Mason said, "If Your Honor please, that's like the man who tells about shooting a deer at three hundred yards and says that the deer fell right by a certain oak tree, that if you don't believe him, he'll point out the oak tree, because it's still standing there and that will substantiate his story."

"You question Mr. Boles' story?"

"Very much," Mason said.

"But you certainly can't question the fact that this evidence is most important evidence. This is evidence which should have been in the hands of the authorities."

"Evidence of what, Your Honor?"

"Here is the driving license of Jackson Eagan."

"Yes, Your Honor."

"Do you mean to say that is not important?"

"I fail to see why," Mason said.

"That would serve as an identification. An attempt has been made by the police to have this corpse identified. So far no identification has been made other than a tentative identification of Jackson Eagan."

"But Jackson Eagan is dead," Mason said. "He died two years before this case ever came up."

"How do you know he died?" Judge Cadwell said. "Here is a contract that was signed, apparently by the decedent, a contract for the rental of that automobile. Do you claim these matters are not important, Mr. Mason?"

"No, sir."

"You certainly understand that they are matters of evidence?"

"Yes, Your Honor."

"As an officer of this Court, as an attorney at law, it is your duty to submit any matter of evidence, any physical matter which you have in your possession to the authorities. To suppress willfully or conceal any evidence of this sort is not only a violation of law but is a violation of your duties as an attorney."

Mason met the judge's eyes. "I'll meet that charge, Your Honor, when it is properly made, at the proper time and at the proper place."

Judge Cadwell's face turned a deep purple. "You are intimating that I have no right to bring this matter up?"

"I am stating, Your Honor, that I will meet that charge at the proper time and in the proper place."

"I don't know whether this constitutes a contempt of Court or not," Judge Cadwell said, "but it certainly constitutes a breach of your professional duty."

"That's Your Honor's opinion," Mason said. "If you w.
to hold me for contempt I'll get a writ of habeas corpus and meet the contempt charge. If you wish to cite me for unprofessional conduct, I will meet that charge at the proper time and in the proper place.

"In the meantime, may I suggest to the Court that a defendant is on trial in this Court, that any intimation on the part of the Court that his counsel has been guilty of any breach of ethics might well be held against the defendant by the jury, and that it is the duty of the Court to refrain from expressing any opinion as to the action of counsel in this matter."

Judge Cadwell took a deep breath. "Mr. Mason," he said, "I am going to do everything I can to see that the rights of the defendant are not prejudiced by the conduct of his counsel. However, I can assure you that, as far as this Court is concerned, I feel that you have forfeited the right to the respect of the Court. Quite apparently you, as an attorney, have endeavored to condone a felony and you have suppressed evidence. As far as the witness Boles is concerned, I assume that he has endeavored to make atonement by going to the authorities and telling his story, but apparently you have done nothing."

"I have done nothing," Mason said, "except try to protect the rights of my client, and I'm going to try to protect them to the best of my ability."

"Well, you certainly have a different idea of the professional duties of an attorney than I do," Judge Cadwell snapped. "That is all. I'll think the matter over during the noon adjournment. I may decide to take some action when Court has reconvened."

Chapter 18

Perry Mason, Della Street, Marilyn Keith, and Paul Drake sat in a booth in the little restaurant where Mason usually ate lunch when he had a case in court.

"Well," Paul Drake asked, "just where does that leave us, Perry?"

"Out on the end of a limb," Mason admitted. "It's perjury, and it's the damnedest, most clever perjury I've ever encountered."

"He's clever," Marilyn Keith said, "frighteningly so, and he's powerful."

Mason nodded. "He's had legal training. He's been a lobbyist. He doubtless knows every trick of cross-examination that I do. It's his word against mine and he's manufactured a story that seems to have all sorts of factual corroboration."

"What about his withholding evidence?" Drake asked.

"Sure," Mason said. "He admits it. So what? The district attorney won't do a thing to him. He won't even slap his wrists. He'll tell him he *should* have surrendered the evidence to the district attorney's office, and not to do it again, but that's all.

"The devil of it is," Mason went on, "that it puts the defendant in such a hell of a position. It's a clever story. It has aroused a certain amount of sympathy for Ted Balfour on the part of the jurors. If Ted goes on the stand and tells approximately that same story, says that he relied on the advice of the older man, some members on that jury are going to vote for acquittal. They'll finally reach some kind of a compromise verdict."

154

"How good is your point about this once-in-jeopardy business?" Drake asked.

"Damn good," Mason said. "In the right kind of a case, the Supreme Court is pretty apt to go all the way."

"Well, it would make a terrific case," Drake said, "if we could only get a little more evidence about the collector coming to call."

Mason said, "The worst of it is, the story sounds so plausible that I'm almost believing it myself."

"Is there anything you can do?" Marilyn Keith asked him.

"I have one weapon," Mason said. "It's a powerful weapon. But sometimes it's hard to wield it because you don't know just where to grab hold of it."

"What weapon is that?" Della Street asked.

"The truth," Mason said.

They ate for a while in silence.

"You'll cross-examine him?" Paul Drake asked.

"I'll cross-examine him. It won't do any good."

"If his story had been true—well, what about it, Perry, what about concealing evidence?"

"As I told Judge Cadwell, I'll cross that bridge when I come to it," Mason said. "Right now I'm trying to think of the best way to protect young Balfour. Of course no matter what anyone says, that driving license of Jackson Eagan doesn't prove a thing. It shows a thumbprint on the driving license and it's not the thumbprint of the corpse." Mason took from his pocket a set of ten fingerprints. "These are the fingerprints of the corpse. This is the thumbprint on the driving license of Jackson Eagan. You can see that they don't compare at all."

"Jackson Eagan was buried," Paul Drake said. "But no one really identified the body. The body had been shipped from Yucatán, Mexico. The story was that it had been identified down there by the widow."

"Just what were the circumstances?" Mason asked.

"Eagan was a writer. He was on a trip getting local color. No one knows exactly how he died. Probably heart failure, or something of that sort. A party of archeologists stumbled on his body. They notified the authorities. The body was taken in to Merida in Yucatán, and the widow was notified by telegram. She flew down to identify the body and bring it home for the funeral. Naturally under the circumstances, the funeral was held with a closed coffin.''

Mason said thoughtfully, ''Just supposing the widow wanted her freedom and perhaps wanted to collect some insurance. It was quite a temptation for her to swear that the body was that of her husband.''

''Of course we get back to that thumbprint,'' Drake said, ''but when you look at the signature on this contract to rent the car, the signatures certainly tally.''

''They certainly seem to be the same signature,'' Mason said. ''Paul, how about the application for a driving license signed by Guthrie Balfour? Did you get that?''

Drake said, ''I wired for a certified copy of Guthrie Balfour's last application for a driving license. It should be here any minute. I was hoping it would come in this morning. I feel certain that it must arrive in the late morning mail. One of my operatives will bring it up to court as soon as it comes in.''

''I want it as soon as I can get it,'' Mason said.

''Do you have any plans for this afternoon's session?'' Drake asked.

Mason shook his head, said, ''Something like this catches you flatfooted. I had anticipated that they would try to make things tough for me, but I didn't think I'd have someone get on the stand and commit deliberate perjury like that.

''Paul, the number of that taxicab in which we took the ride was 647. I want to try and find the driver of the cab. I doubt if he'd remember anything that would be of help, but at least we can check. He should remember the occasion, even if he can't identify Boles.''

''I'll have my men round him up,'' Drake said.

''Well,'' Mason announced, ''I'll just have to go back

156

there and take it on the chin. I've absorbed lots of punishment before and I guess I can take a little more.''

"Of course you have the advantage of knowing what actually happened," Della Street said. "Eagan was shot by Guthrie Balfour. He telephoned Florence Ingle and admitted that.''

"Well, why not use that?" Marilyn Keith asked. "Why not just go ahead on that basis and—?''

Mason smiled and shook his head. "No can do.''

"Why not?''

"Because Guthrie Balfour told her over the telephone that he had killed this man. He said the killing was accidental, that the gun had gone off in a struggle.''

"Can't you use that?''

"No.''

"Why not?''

"Because that's hearsay. If we had Guthrie Balfour here, we could put him on the stand and question him, and, if he told a different story, we could then put Florence Ingle on the stand and impeach him by having Florence tell what he had said. But the law won't let a witness simply testify to what someone else has said over the telephone.''

"It let Banner Boles testify to what Ted said over the telephone!" Marilyn exclaimed indignantly.

"Sure," Mason said, "because Ted's the defendant. You can always show any adverse statement that has been made by a defendant, but, unfortunately for us, Guthrie Balfour isn't a defendant. The technical rules of evidence prevent us getting at what we want.''

"And what does Guthrie Balfour say about it?" Marilyn asked.

"Nobody knows," Mason said. "Guthrie headed back to his base camp. How about your men? Any luck, Paul?''

Drake shook his head. "Guthrie Balfour was in Chihuahua very briefly. He headed back for the Tarahumare country somewhere. He was only in Chihuahua long enough to telephone you and put his wife on a plane to come in and see you. Then he was off again. And my best guess, Perry, is that this expedition of his may have started out as a little archeological exploration, but it has now developed into a game of hide-and-seek. I don't think he intends to have anybody catch up with him until after this case is all over. Of course, in justice to him, you have to remember that as far as he's concerned it's still only a hit-and-run case. He feels nothing very much can happen to Ted—a fine or a suspended sentence."

Mason signed the luncheon check, said, "Well, we may just as well go back and face the music. We may not like the tune but we'll dance to it."

Chapter 19

After Court had been reconvened at two o'clock, Roger Farris said, "I have no more questions of this witness. You may cross-examine, Mr. Mason."

Mason said, "Do you remember an occasion a short time ago when you telephoned me at my office, Mr. Boles?"

"Perfectly," Boles said affably.

"You came up to my office and said you had something to tell me?"

"Yes, sir."

"And I asked you to talk to me in my office and you said you'd prefer not to do so?"

"Yes, sir, that's quite right."

"And we went out and rode around in a taxicab together?"

"Yes, sir."

"You remember that, do you?"

"Certainly, sir. I not only remember it, but I took the precaution of jotting down the number of the taxicab so that the driver could bear me out in case you tried to confuse me on cross-examination or tried to deny that I gave you these papers."

"You gave them to me while we were in the taxicab?"

"That's right."

"And what did you tell me when you gave me the papers?"

"The same story that I have told on the witness stand today."

"At that time, didn't you tell me that Mr. Guthrie Balfour had told you that *he* had done the shooting and that the dead

159

man had been someone who was in the Sleepy Hollow Motel?''

Boles looked at Mason with absolute, utter incredulity. ''Do you mean that *I* told you *that*?'' he asked.

''Didn't you?'' Mason asked.

''Good heavens, no!'' Boles said. ''Don't be absurd, Mr. Mason. Why in the world should I tell you that? Why Guthrie Balfour was . . . why he was on his way to Mexico. I put him on the train personally.''

''What about the company airplane? Wasn't that subsequently picked up in Phoenix?''

''Either Phoenix or Tucson, I think,'' Boles said. ''But that was at a later date. One of the company employees flew down there on a matter of some importance and then I believe left the plane, as he took a commercial airline on East. I don't know, but I can look up the company records, in case you're interested, Mr. Mason. I'm quite satisfied the company records will show that to be the case.''

''I dare say,'' Mason said drily.

There was a moment's pause.

''Did you go out to the Sleepy Hollow Motel on the evening of the nineteenth or the twentieth?'' Mason asked.

Boles shook his head, and said, ''I wasn't anywhere near there. No one knew anything about this car at the Sleepy Hollow Motel until I believe the police picked it up, by tracing a key. I don't know about those things. I think the police could tell you, Mr. Mason.''

''When did you last see Guthrie Balfour?'' Mason asked.

''When he took the train at the Arcade Station.''

''And you haven't seen him since?''

''No, sir.''

''Or heard from him?''

''Yes, sir. I've heard from him.''

''When did you hear from him?''

''I believe that was the day that Mr. Balfour was tried the first time before the first jury. I believe that's the date but I'm not certain. Mr. Guthrie Balfour had been back in

160

the mountains somewhere. He came in briefly for supplies and learned of the defendant's arrest. He telephoned me and told me that he had just talked with you on the telephone, and that his wife Dorla was flying up to get in touch with you."

There was an air of complete candor about the witness which carried conviction.

"You recognized his voice?"

"Of course."

"That's all for the moment," Mason said. "I may wish to recall this witness."

"You may step down," Judge Cadwell said. "Call your next witness, Mr. Prosecutor."

"Florence Ingle," the prosecutor announced.

Florence Ingle came forward, was sworn, gave her name and address.

"You have been subpoenaed as a witness for the defense?" Farris asked.

"Yes, sir."

"I will ask you whether you saw the defendant on the evening of September nineteenth?"

"I did," she answered in a low voice.

"What was his condition?"

"When?"

"At the time you last saw him?"

"At the time I last saw him he had quite evidently been drinking."

"Did he tell you anything at that time about being in debt?"

"Yes, sir. It was a little before that time . . . the evening of September nineteenth."

"What was the conversation, please? But first let me ask you, who was present at that time?"

"Quite a number of people were present at the house, but they were not present when we had the conversation; that is, they were not where they could hear the conversation."

"Just the two of you were present?"

"Yes, sir."

"And what did the defendant tell you?"

"He asked if he could borrow twenty thousand dollars. He told me that he was in debt, that he had run up some gambling debts and that the persons with whom he had been dealing telephoned him and threatened to send a collector unless he made immediate payment."

"Did he say anything about what he thought the collector wanted?"

"Yes, he said those collectors got pretty rough the first time, that sometimes they took people on a one-way ride, but that they beat up anyone who welched on a bet."

"And did he tell you what he intended to do if a collector tried to beat him up?"

"He said he was going to defend himself."

"Did he say how?"

"He said, 'With a gun.' "

"You may inquire," Farris said.

"Did you have any talk with Guthrie Balfour, the defendant's uncle, on that day?" Mason asked.

"Objected to as incompetent, irrelevant, and immaterial, not proper cross-examination," Farris said.

"I would like to have an answer to the question, Your Honor. I think that there is an entire transaction here which should be viewed as a unit."

"Certainly not as a unit," Farris said. "We have no objection to Mr. Mason asking this witness about any conversation she may have had with the defendant in this case. We have no objection to Mr. Mason asking about any matters which were brought up in connection with the conversation on which the witness was questioned on her direct examination, but we certainly do not intend to permit any evidence as to some conversation she may have had with the uncle of the defendant which was not within the presence of the defendant and which, for all we know, has absolutely nothing to do with the issues involved in this case.

162

"If there is any such conversation and if it is pertinent, it is part of the defendant's case. This witness is subpoenaed as a witness for the defense. Counsel can examine her as much as he wants to about any conversation with Mr. Guthrie Balfour when he calls her as his own witness. At that time we will of course object to any conversation which took place without the presence of the defendant or which has no bearing upon the present case.

"If a person could prove a point by any such procedure as this, there would be no point in swearing a witness. Anyone could get on the stand and tell about some conversation had with some person who was not under oath."

"I think that's quite right, Mr. Mason," Judge Cadwell said. "The Court wishes to be perfectly fair and impartial in the matter, but you can't show any evidence of a conversation with some person who is not a party to the proceedings, and you can't frame such a question as part of your cross-examination. The Court will permit you the most searching cross-examination as to this particular conversation the witness has testified to. The objection is sustained."

"No further questions," Mason said.

"We will call Mrs. Guthrie Balfour to the stand," Farris said.

While Mrs. Balfour was walking forward, Paul Drake stepped up to the bar and caught Mason's eye. He handed Mason a paper and whispered, "This is a certified photostatic copy of Guthrie Balfour's application for a driving license."

Mason nodded, spread out the paper, glanced at it, looked at it again, then folded the paper.

Dorla Balfour was making quite an impression on the jury. The trim lines of her figure, the expressive brown eyes, the vivacious yet subdued manner with which she indicated that her natural vitality was being suppressed out of deference to the solemnity of the occasion, made the jurors prepare to like her right from the start.

She gave her name and address to the court reporter, adjusting herself in the witness chair with a pert little wiggle, raised her lashes, looked at the deputy district attorney, then at the jury, then lowered her lashes demurely.

At that moment there was a commotion in the courtroom, and Hamilton Burger, the big grizzly bear of a district attorney, came striding purposefully into the courtroom.

It needed only a glance at the smug triumph of his countenance to realize that word of Perry Mason's discomfiture had been relayed to him, and he had entered the case personally in order to be in at the kill.

Too many times he had seen Mason, by the use of startling ingenuity, squeeze his way out of some seemingly impossible situation. Now he had waited until he was certain Mason had shot all the arrows from his quiver before entering court. It was apparent to everyone that Dorla Balfour would be the last witness, and then Mason would be forced to make a decision. Either he would put the defendant on the stand, or he would not. If he put the defendant on the stand and the defendant's story coincided with that of Banner Boles, the defendant might have a good chance of showing self-defense. But in that case, Mason would run the risk of an admission of unprofessional conduct and be branded for withholding evidence Boles had given him. If the defendant's story should differ from Boles' testimony, there was not one chance in a hundred the jury would believe it.

Farris, apparently trying to appear in the best possible light before his chief, said, "Mrs. Balfour, do you remember the evening of the nineteenth of September of this year?"

"Very well," she said.

"Did you have any conversation with the defendant on that day?"

"I did, yes, sir."

"When?"

"In the evening."

"Where?"

"At a party given by Mrs. Ingle for my husband."

"That was in the nature of a going-away party?"

164

"Yes, sir."

"Your husband took the train that night?"

"Yes, sir."

"And did you take the train?"

"Yes, sir, I was to have accompanied my husband as far as the station at Pasadena. However, at the last minute he asked me to go all the way with him."

"Well, never mind that," the prosecutor said. "I'm just trying to fix the time and place of the conversation. Now who was present at this conversation?"

"The one I had with the defendant?"

"Yes."

"Just the defendant and I were present. That is, there were other people in the group but he took me to one side."

"And what did he say to you?"

"He told me that he had incurred some gambling debts; that they were debts on which he didn't dare to welch; that he had been plunging because he had got in pretty deep and he had to make good or he was threatened with personal danger. He said that they had told him a collector was coming, that these collectors were sort of a goon squad who would beat him up and—well, that he *had* to have some money."

"Did he ask you for money?"

"Not me. But he asked me if, while I was on the train, I couldn't intercede for him with my husband and get my husband to let him have twenty thousand dollars."

"You may inquire," Farris said.

"And you did intercede with your husband?" Mason asked.

"Not then. I did later on."

"How much later on?"

"Well, Mr. Mason, you understand I was supposed to get off the train at Pasadena, and then Guthrie asked me to go on with him all the way. He said that he felt uneasy, that he felt that something perhaps was going to happen. He asked me to accompany him."

"And you did?" Mason asked.

"Objected to as incompetent, irrelevant, and immaterial. Not proper cross-examination in that it has nothing to do with the conversation concerning which this witness has testified. We are perfectly willing to let Mr. Mason explore all of the facts in connection with that conversation, but any conversation which subsequently took place between this witness and her husband would be incompetent, irrelevant, and immaterial. It would be hearsay, and we object to it."

"Sustained," Judge Cadwell said.

"Didn't you actually get off the train at Pasadena?" Mason asked.

"Objected to as incompetent, irrelevant, and immaterial. Not proper cross-examination."

"I will permit the question," Judge Cadwell said. "I am going to give the defense every opportunity for a searching cross-examination. The question of what this witness may have said to her husband is one thing, but any of the circumstances surrounding the conversation that was had on this occasion may be gone into. Answer the question."

"Certainly not," she said.

"Didn't you go to the Sleepy Hollow Motel on that evening?"

"Oh, Your Honor," Roger Farris protested. "The vice of this is now perfectly apparent. This is an attempt to befuddle the issues in this case. It is also a dastardly attack on this witness. It makes no difference what she did. She has testified only to her conversation."

"She testified that she went on the train with her husband," Judge Cadwell said. "The Court wishes to give the defense every latitude. I think I will permit an answer to this question."

"Did you go to the Sleepy Hollow Motel?" Mason asked.

"Certainly not," she flared at him. "And you have no

right to ask such a question, Mr. Mason. You know perfectly good and well that I didn't do any such thing.''

"Do you remember an occasion when your husband telephoned me from Chihuahua?" Mason asked.

"Certainly," she said.

"You were with him at that time?"

"Yes."

"And that is when you returned from Chihuahua?"

"Yes."

"That was the occasion when the defendant was on trial for manslaughter?"

"It was the day after the trial; that is, it was the day of the trial, but after the trial had been concluded."

"And you did catch a plane from Chihuahua?"

"I chartered a plane from Chihuahua and was taken to El Paso. I caught a plane at El Paso and came here. Yes."

"And you saw me the next morning?"

"Yes."

"And you were with your husband when he telephoned?"

"Oh, Your Honor," Farris said, "here we go, on and on and on. This is the vice of opening the door on cross-examination. I don't know what counsel is expecting to prove. I do know that we would like to confine the issues in this case to a simple question of fact. I object to this question on the ground that it is not proper cross-examination, that it's incompetent, irrelevant, and immaterial."

"I am going to permit the answer to this one question," Judge Cadwell said. "I think myself this is going far afield, but it may have a bearing on possible bias on the part of the witness.

"The question, Mrs. Balfour, is whether you were with your husband at the time he telephoned Mr. Mason on that date."

"I was. Yes, sir."

"And," Mason went on, "were you subsequently with him when he telephoned to Mr. Banner Boles?"

"I am not going to object to this question," Roger Farris said, "on the sole and specific understanding that it is not to be used to open a door for a long involved line of extraneous questions. I don't think counsel is entitled to go on a fishing expedition."

"The Court feels that this line of questioning has certainly gone far enough," Judge Cadwell said. "The Court wishes to give the defense every opportunity for a cross-examination. Answer the question, Mrs. Balfour. Were you with your husband when he telephoned Mr. Banner Boles?"

"Yes, sir."

"Well then," Mason said, getting to his feet, "perhaps Mrs. Balfour, you wouldn't mind turning to the jury and explaining to them how it could possibly be that you journeyed on the train to El Paso with a corpse, that you spent some time in Chihuahua with a corpse, that you were with a corpse when he telephoned Mr. Banner Boles?"

"What in the world do you mean?" she snapped, before the stupefied Roger Farris could even so much as interpose an objection.

"Simply this," Mason said, snapping open the paper he was holding. "The right thumbprint of your husband Guthrie Balfour which is shown on this certified copy of an application for a driver's license is an exact copy of the right thumbprint of the dead man, as disclosed by the coroner's record. The man who was found with this bullet in his brain, the man who was supposedly the victim of this hit-and-run episode, that man was your husband, Guthrie Balfour. Now perhaps you can explain how it happened that you spent this time with a dead man?"

"It can't be," she said vehemently. "I was with my husband. I—"

"Let me see that thumbprint," Judge Cadwell snapped.

Mason brought up the thumbprint.

"And let me take a look at the exhibit showing the fingerprints of the dead man," Judge Cadwell said.

For a long moment he compared the two prints.

"Would the prosecution like to look at this evidence?" Judge Cadwell asked.

"No, Your Honor," Hamilton Burger said smiling. "We are too familiar with counsel's dramatic tricks to be impressed by them."

"You'd better be impressed by this one," Judge Cadwell said, "because unless there's some mistake in the exhibit it is quite apparent that the prints are the same."

"Then it is quite apparent that there has been some trickery in connection with the exhibits," Hamilton Burger said.

"Now if the Court please," Mason went on, "I am suddenly impressed by certain signatures on the record of the Sleepy Hollow Motel, which I have had photostated. It is evident that one of these signatures, that of Jackson Eagan, is similar to the signature on the driver's license issued to Jackson Eagan. However, I would like time to have a handwriting expert compare the signature of the man who signed his name 'Jackson Eagan' with the handwriting of Banner Boles. I think, if the Court please, I begin to see the pattern of what must have happened on the night of September nineteenth."

"Now just a moment, just a moment," Hamilton Burger shouted. "I object to any such statement by counsel. I object to such a motion. I object to the Court permitting any such statement in front of a jury. I charge counsel with misconduct because of that remark, and I ask the Court to admonish the jury to disregard it."

Judge Cadwell turned to the openmouthed jurors. "The jurors will not be influenced by any remarks made by counsel for either side," he said. "The Court, however, of its own motion, is going to take an adjournment for an hour, during which time certain records will be examined. I am particularly anxious to have a qualified fingerprint

169

expert examine this unquestioned similarity between a thumbprint of Guthrie Balfour on this application for a driving license, and the right thumbprint of the dead man who is the decedent in this case. Court will take a one-hour recess, during which time the jurors are not to converse with anyone about this case, not to discuss it among yourselves, and not to form or express any opinion. Court will take a recess."

Judge Cadwell banged down his gavel, rose from the bench, and said, "I'd like to see counsel for both sides in chambers."

Chapter 20

In Judge Cadwell's chambers an irate Hamilton Burger said, "What I want to find out first is why Perry Mason withheld and concealed this evidence."

"Well, what *I* want to find out," Judge Cadwell said, "is Mr. Mason's theory of what happened in this case."

"With all due respect to Your Honor," Hamilton Burger said, "I think Mr. Mason's explanation should come first. I don't think he is entitled to appear here in good standing until he has purged himself of this charge."

"With all due respect to your opinion," Judge Cadwell snapped, "this is a first-degree murder case. Mr. Mason seems to have a theory which accounts for this startling fingerprint evidence. I want to hear that theory."

Mason grinned at the discomfited district attorney and said, "I think it's quite simple, Your Honor. The rented car which was found at the Sleepy Hollow Motel was a car which had apparently been rented by Jackson Eagan, despite the fact that the records show that Jackson Eagan has been dead for some two years.

"That car actually was rented by Banner Boles. Obviously Boles must have been in Mexico when the body of Jackson Eagan was discovered. He took charge of Eagan's papers. He knew that Eagan would have no further use for his driving license. He noticed that the physical description fitted his own physical description. Occasionally, when he was working on a job where he didn't want to use his own name, or when he wanted to go on a philandering expedition, he knew that by renting a car and using the Eagan name, with the

Eagan driving license as a means of identification, there was no way his real identity could be traced.

"I could have proved that Guthrie Balfour got off the train to follow his wife if the rules of evidence had permitted me to show a conversation Guthrie Balfour had with Florence Ingle. I couldn't show that in court, but I can tell Your Honor that that's what happened.

"Dorla Balfour was having an affair with none other than Banner Boles of Balfour Allied Associates."

"Oh, bosh!" Hamilton Burger snapped.

Judge Cadwell frowned. "We'll let Mr. Mason finish, Mr. Burger. Then you may have your turn."

Mason said, "Florence Ingle had a conversation over the telephone with Guthrie Balfour. He was ready to divorce Dorla, he wanted to get evidence on her, so he wouldn't have to pay excessive alimony. She got off the train, as planned, at Pasadena and Guthrie Balfour got off the train as he had planned it all along, getting off on the other side of the train. He hurried to a car which he had rented earlier in the day and left there at the station so he could jump in it and drive off. He followed his wife to the place of rendezvous. He secured an adjoining cabin, set up a very sensitive microphone which recorded everything that took place in the adjoining cabin on tape. Then Dorla went home to get her suitcase and planned to return to spend the night.

"The tape recorder recorded all of the words that were spoken in the other cabin, but because of the extreme sensitivity of the microphone there was a certain distortion and Guthrie Balfour still didn't know the identity of the man who was dating his wife. After Dorla left, he determined to enter the cabin, act the part of the outraged husband, and get a statement.

"He entered the cabin. The lights were low. Banner Boles, who occupied that cabin, was waiting for Dorla to return. To his surprise and consternation, he saw the husband, who was not only the man whose home he had invaded, but who was one of the men he worked for.

172

"He knew that Guthrie Balfour hadn't as yet recognized him, and he didn't dare to give Balfour the chance. He dazzled Balfour by directing the beam of a powerful flashlight in the man's eyes. Then, having blinded Balfour, he threw a chair and launched an attack, hoping that he could knock Balfour out and make his escape from the cabin before his identity could be discovered.

"Balfour drew his gun, and in the struggle the gun went off. That was when Banner Boles, acting with the rare presence of mind which has made him a skillful troubleshooter, sank face down on the floor, pretended to be mortally wounded, then lay still.

"In a panic, Guthrie Balfour ran out, jumped into his rented car and drove home. He didn't know what to do. He knew that his shot was going to result in a scandal. He wanted to avoid that at all costs. Then it occurred to him that no one really knew he had gone off the train, except the man whom he had every reason to believe was lying dead in the Sleepy Hollow Motel.

"In the meantime, Banner Boles got to his feet, ran to the telephone booth, and put through a call to Dorla at her home telling her exactly what had happened."

"You know this for a fact?" Judge Cadwell asked.

"I know most of the facts. I am making one or two factual deductions from the things I know."

"Using a crystal ball," Hamilton Burger sneered.

"So," Mason went on, "Guthrie Balfour planned to take the company plane to Phoenix, board the train there, and pretend that nothing had happened. He rang up Florence Ingle and asked her to go to Phoenix on a commercial plane and fly the company plane back. He felt that he could trust Florence Ingle. She was the only one in whom he confided. However, he overlooked the fact that Dorla Balfour was at home, that she had been warned that her perfidy had been discovered, that her house of cards was about to come tumbling down. She concealed herself. As soon as she heard his voice, she tiptoed to a point of vantage where she could hear what he was saying. While she was listening to that phone conversation, she suddenly knew a way by which she could extricate herself from her predicament.

"So Dorla waited until her husband had hung up, then rushed to him in apparent surprise and said, 'Why, Guthrie, I thought you were on the train. What happened?'

"Balfour had probably placed Ted's gun on the stand by the telephone. Dorla, still acting the part of the surprised but faithful wife, with her left arm around her husband, picked up the gun and probably said, 'Why, dear, what's this?'

"Then she took the gun and shot him in the head without warning.

"Then she telephone Banner Boles at whatever place he had told her he'd be waiting, and asked him to come at once. So he grabbed a cab and joined Dorla. Then he took charge. Between them they got the idea of banging the body around so that the features would be unrecognizable, making it appear to be a hit-and-run accident and framing Ted with the whole thing, knowing that in case that didn't work they could use Florence Ingle to make it appear Guthrie Balfour was the murderer and that he had resorted to flight.

"So Boles returned the car that he had rented in the name of Jackson Eagan and left it there at the motel. He hoped the hit-and-run theory would work and the corpse would remain unidentified, but if things didn't work another anonymous tip to the police would bring Jackson Eagan into the picture. Boles wanted to have a complete supply of red herrings available in case his scheme encountered difficulties anywhere.

"Thereafter, as things worked out, it was relatively simple. Banner Boles returned to the Florence Ingle party. He managed to drug a drink so that Ted Balfour hardly knew what he was doing. Boles intended to take charge of Ted at that point, but Marilyn Keith saw Ted in an apparently intoxicated condition, so she drove him home and put him to bed.

"However, after she had gone home, the conspirators got the car Ted had been driving, took it out and ran it over

Guthrie Balfour's body, smashed up the headlight, left enough clues so that the police would be certain to investigate, and then, in order to be certain, arranged that there would be a witness, a Myrtle Anne Haley, who would tie in the accident directly with Ted Balfour. They arranged to have an anonymous tip send the police out to look at Ted's car.

"It only remained for the conspirators to take the company plane, fly it to Phoenix and get aboard the train, using the railroad ticket which they had taken from Balfour's body. Since Dorla had overheard her husband's conversation with Florence Ingle, she knew that Florence Ingle would go to Phoenix and bring the plane back, feeling certain that she was helping Guthrie Balfour in his deception.

"Of course, the planning in this was part of the masterminding of Banner Boles. That's been his job for years, to think fast in situations where another man would be panic-stricken, to mix up the evidence so that it would be interpreted about any way he wanted to have it interpreted. This was probably one of the highlights of his career.

"He crossed the border, taking out a tourist card as Guthrie Balfour. He was very careful not to telephone anyone who could detect the deception. For instance, he never telephoned Florence Ingle to thank her for what she had done or to tell her that everything had worked out according to schedule. He didn't dare to do that because she would have recognized that the voice was not that of Guthrie Balfour. On the other hand, since *I* don't know Guthrie Balfour and had never talked with him, Boles was able to ring me up, disguise his voice slightly, tell me that he was Guthrie Balfour and that he was sending his wife to see me."

"That's all very interesting," Judge Cadwell said. "How are you going to prove it?"

"*I'm* not going to prove it," Mason said, "but I think that the police can prove it if they will go to the unit in the Sleepy Hollow Motel which was occupied by Banner Boles when he registered under the name of Jackson Eagan, and I think they'll find there's a small bullet hole in the floor which has hitherto been unnoticed. I think that if the police dig in there, they'll find another bullet discharged from that gun belonging to Ted Balfour."

"Very, very interesting," Judge Cadwell said. "I take it, Mr. District Attorney, that you will put the necessary machinery in motion to see that this case is investigated at once."

"If Mr. Mason is entirely finished," Hamilton Burger said angrily, "I'll now ask the Court to remember that I'm to have my inning. I want to ask Mr. Mason how it happened he was in possession of this evidence which he was concealing from the police."

"I wasn't concealing it from the police," Mason said. "I was waiting for an opportunity to present it in such a manner that a murderer could be apprehended.

"For your information, when we were in that taxicab Banner Boles confessed the whole thing to me, except, of course, that he didn't admit that he was the Beau Brummell who had been making love to Dorla Balfour. He offered me a fee of more than a hundred thousand dollars to see that the facts didn't come out in court. Under the circumstances, I was entitled to hold the evidence until the moment when a disclosure would bring the real criminal to justice. I wasn't concealing any evidence. I was waiting to produce it at the right time.

"However, Banner Boles got on the stand, committed perjury, and forced my hand. I had to surrender the evidence before I was ready."

"Your word against that of Banner Boles," Hamilton Burger said.

"Exactly," Mason told him, smiling. "My word against that of a perjurer and accessory to a murder."

"How are you going to prove that?" Hamilton Burger snapped. "You've come up here with a cockeyed theory, but how are you going to prove it?"

"*You* can prove it if you get busy and recover that extra bullet," Mason said. "And you can prove it if you ask him how it happened that, under oath, he swore to a conversation with a man whose fingerprints show that he had been dead for some time before the conversation took place. You can also prove it by getting in touch with the Mexican government and finding the tourist card that was issued to Guthrie Balfour. You'll find that that was in the handwriting of Banner Boles and you'll find that when Banner Boles left Mexico, he surrendered that tourist card properly countersigned."

Judge Cadwell smiled at the district attorney. "I think, Mr. District Attorney," he said, "most of the logic, as well as *all* of the equities, are in favor of Perry Mason's position."

Chapter 21

Perry Mason, Della Street, Marilyn Keith, Paul Drake, and Ted Balfour gathered for a brief, jubilant session in the witness room adjacent to Judge Cadwell's courtroom.

"Remember now," Mason cautioned Ted Balfour, "at the moment you are jubilant because you have been released. But your uncle has been murdered. You had an affection for him. You're going to be interviewed by the press. You're going to be photographed, and you're going through quite an ordeal."

Balfour nodded.

"And then," Mason said, "you're going to have to get in touch with your Uncle Addison Balfour and explain to him what happened, and you're going to have to see that Marilyn Keith is reinstated."

"You leave that to me," Balfour said. "I'm going to have a talk with him within thirty minutes of the time I leave this courthouse."

A knock sounded on the door. Mason frowned. "I'd hoped the newspaper reporters wouldn't find us here. I didn't want to face them until we were ready. Well, we'll have to take it now. I don't want them to think we're hiding."

Mason flung the door open.

However, it wasn't a newspaper reporter who stood on the threshold, but the bailiff of Judge Cadwell's court who had arranged, in the first place, to have the witness room made available for the conference.

"I don't like to disturb you, Mr. Mason," he said, "but it's a most important telephone call."

178

"Just a moment," Mason told the others. "You wait here. I'll be right back."

"There's a phone in this next room," the bailiff said.

"Better come along, Paul," Mason said. "This may be something you'll have to work on. You, too, Della."

Della Street and Paul Drake hurried out to stand by Mason's shoulder as Mason picked up the receiver.

"Hello," Mason said.

A thin, reedy voice came over the line. "Mr. Mason, I guess you recognize my voice. I'm Addison Balfour. Please don't interrupt. I haven't much strength.

"I'm sorry that I was deceived about you. I shouldn't have listened to others. I should have known that a man doesn't build up the reputation you have built up unless he has what it takes.

"I'm all broken up about Guthrie but there's no help for that now. We all have to go sometime.

"You have done a remarkable piece of work. You have, incidentally, saved the Balfour Allied Associates from a great scandal, as well as a great financial loss."

"You know what went on in court?" Mason asked.

"Certainly I know," Addison Balfour snapped. "I also know what went on in the judge's chambers. I may be sick, but I'm not mentally incapacitated. I've had reports coming in every half-hour. Don't think I'm a damn fool just because I acted like one when I let Banner Boles talk me into firing you, so he could try to get Mortimer Dean Howland to take over Ted's defense.

"You send your bill to the Balfour Allied Associates for a hundred and fifty thousand dollars for legal services, and you tell that secretary of mine to get the hell back here on the job. I'm going to make a very substantial cash settlement with her to compensate her for the defamation of character connected with her temporary discharge. As for my nephew, you can tell him to stop worrying about his gambling debt now. I think he's learned his lesson.

"And if you want to cheer up a dying old man, you people

will get out here as soon as you can and tell me that I'm forgiven. That's all. Good-by.''

Addison Balfour hung up the phone at the other end of the line.

Mason turned to find the anxious faces of both Paul Drake and Della Street.

"Who was it?" Della Street asked.

"Addison Balfour," Mason told her. "He's anxious to make amends. He wants us out there as soon as possible."

"Well, then we'd better get out there as soon as possible," Paul Drake said. "In fact, it would be a swell thing from a standpoint of public relations if the newspaper reporters had to interview us *after* we got out there."

"We won't be able to leave the building undetected," Mason said. "We can tell the reporters that we're going out there, but we're going to be interviewed within a few minutes, Paul."

Mason pushed open the door to the witness room, then suddenly stepped back and gently closed the door.

"We'll wait a minute or two before we go in," he said, grinning. "I think the two people in there are discussing something that's damned important—to them."

About the Author

Erle Stanley Gardner is the king of American mystery fiction. A criminal lawyer, he filled his mystery masterpieces with intricate, fascinating, ever-twisting plots. Challenging, clever, and full of surprises, these are whodunits in the best tradition. During his lifetime, Erle Stanley Gardner wrote 146 books, 85 of which feature Perry Mason.

12   TA-165